"Why did you fabricate such lies?" Tath asked.

His hand slipped around her waist and he drew her to him. While those stony gray eyes pierced through her, he demanded in a deep voice, "Why did you do it, Hilary?"

"I'm sorry. I shouldn't have."

Amusement raised the corners of his mouth into a sardonic smile. "If I'm so damned 'nice' and safe and unappealing, why go to all that trouble? Why tell me such nonsense about your ex-fiancé?" He leaned closer until he was only inches away. "Why?"

"To keep you from doing what you're doing now," she stated honestly.

His warm lips were persistent, silencing her words while he pulled her to him. When he raised his head, she added, "You're a compulsive womanizer and it doesn't mean anything to you when you kiss me."

"You think this doesn't mean anything?" he whispered.

Dear Reader:

June 1983 marked SECOND CHANCE AT LOVE's second birthday—and we have good reason to celebrate! While romantic fiction has continued to grow, SECOND CHANCE AT LOVE has remained in the forefront as an innovative, top-selling romance series. In ever-increasing numbers you, the readers, continue to buy SECOND CHANCE AT LOVE, which you've come to know as the "butterfly books."

During the past two years we've received thousands of letters expressing your enthusiasm for SECOND CHANCE AT LOVE. In particular, many of you have asked: "What happens to the hero and heroine after they get married?"

As we attempted to answer that question, our thoughts led naturally to an exciting new concept—a line of romances based on married love. We're now proud to announce the creation of this new line, coming to you this fall, called TO HAVE AND TO HOLD.

There has never been a series of romances about marriage. As we did with SECOND CHANCE AT LOVE, we're breaking new ground, setting a new precedent. TO HAVE AND TO HOLD romances will be heartwarming, compelling love stories of marriages that remain exciting, adventurous, enriching and, above all, romantic. Each TO HAVE AND TO HOLD romance will bring you two people who love each other deeply. You'll see them struggle with challenges many married couples face. But no matter what happens, their love and commitment will see them through to a brighter future.

We're very enthusiastic about TO HAVE AND TO HOLD, and we hope you will be too. Watch for its arrival this fall. We will, of course, continue to publish six SECOND CHANCE AT LOVE romances every month in addition to our new series. We hope you'll read and enjoy them all!

Warm wishes,

Ellen Edwards

Ellen Edwards
SECOND CHANCE AT LOVE
The Berkley Publishing Group
200 Madison Avenue
New York, N.Y. 10016

SOUTHERN PLEASURES
DAISY LOGAN

**A
SECOND CHANCE AT LOVE
BOOK**

*With love to David,
and with thanks to
Patti and Jim Ladner...*

· 1 ·

New Orleans' afternoon sunshine streamed through the bedroom windows, slanting across the Queen Anne four-poster bed and its white spread. The room was silent. Thick yellow carpet muffled Hilary O'Brien's footsteps as she walked back and forth between the open suitcase and the closet. When she passed the pier glass, she glanced at her image, seeing the curtain of flame-colored hair that fell almost to her shoulders, and wide green eyes above a tailored navy dress. Turning, she hung up two dresses before she gazed across the room to the spot where only a moment ago her dog had slept. She called softly, "Snuffy."

The Yorkshire terrier didn't appear. With a twinge of annoyance, she called louder. "Snuffy!" Circling the room, she looked beneath tables, a dresser, and a yellow-cushioned chaise longue.

"Snuffy, come here!" She glanced in the adjoining yellow tile bathroom. Not seeing her pet, she studied the open bedroom door. Could Snuffy have wandered away? Less than ten minutes ago, Mr. Elliot Compton, comptroller for Justin Mills and the man who had hired her to do three television commercials for his company, had shown her to her room. When he left, Snuffy had curled up to sleep on the floor while Hilary unpacked.

She stepped into the hall and called again, "Snuffy!"

Farther down the hall she heard a growl. Feeling a ripple of alarm because of the terrier's frisky nature, she set out in the direction of the noise.

Halfway down the hall a door stood ajar, and she stepped

into a room that was as masculine as hers was feminine. While she looked around, glimpsing a deep brown and tan decor, shelves of books, and several swimming trophies, one thing riveted her attention.

In the center of the room stood Snuffy, with a blue sweater dangling from his mouth. Beneath his shaggy forehead the dog's brown eyes gazed up at her. While she watched, he placed his front paws on the sweater and tugged.

"No! Oh, Snuffy!" Her heart dropped as she watched strands of yarn pull taut, then snap and begin to unravel. She lunged for him, but the terrier dodged, racing in a circle and barking excitedly before he disappeared under the king-sized bed.

With a hollow feeling in the pit of her stomach, she knelt to raise the brown quilted spread.

"Snuffy, come out from under there!" she ordered in a hoarse whisper. If only she could catch him before someone discovered them! Now she wished she hadn't let Elliot Compton talk her into bringing Snuffy along.

"Come here!"

To her dismay, instead of obeying, he scooted farther from her. Holding the sweater beneath his paws, he released it momentarily. His pink tongue hanging out of his mouth while he panted, he gazed at her.

Snuffy's happy face and her uncomfortable position, resting on her hands and knees as she peered beneath the bed, increased her anger.

"Snuffy, come out!"

There was just enough space between the floor and bed to accommodate the dog. Desperation and anger churned within her. Snuffy looked as if he were laughing at her predicament! Reaching as far as possible, she caught part of the sweater.

Instantly, delighting in the game, Snuffy pulled the sweater out of her fingers and backed farther away. Stretching out on his stomach with his paws securely on his prize, he growled playfully.

Wondering why she'd ever taken in this waif of a dog,

Hilary glared at him. She felt as if he were taunting her. With her cheek pressed against the soft beige carpet, she tried to reach the sweater again.

"Snuffy, when I get you . . ."

"Lose something?" a deep male voice asked.

Startled, Hilary dropped the spread, straightened, and sat back on her heels. Warmth flooded her cheeks as she faced a pair of muscular bare legs. At that moment she would cheerfully have handed Snuffy over to the nearest dogcatcher. Scrambling to move away, she wanted to disappear, to be anywhere else on earth.

Towering above her was a broad-shouldered, deeply tanned man dressed only in a yellow towel. Drops of water glistened on his powerful shoulders, and gleaming dark brown curls clung damply to his high forehead. He held an open bottle of after-shave in one hand, while with the other he reached down to help her to her feet.

Warm fingers closed over her arm, sending an electric current through her flesh, but as soon as she stood, the stranger released her.

Overcome by embarrassment, she was acutely aware of intruding in his room. She guessed this man must be the holder of the swimming trophies that lined the shelves; his body, only a few inches from hers, proclaimed a model of masculine fitness, from his well-muscled legs to his taut stomach and broad chest. As she met his clear gray eyes, which danced with laughter, Hilary was mortified, realizing how ridiculous she had looked with her head and shoulders under the bed. It was terrible to look into the thick-fringed eyes of this compelling man who seemed to fill the room.

Straightening her collar, he said in mocking tones, "It's nicer on my bed than under it."

Her whole body and face burned with shame and confusion. Under any circumstances she would have found this magnetic stranger disconcerting, but to be caught trespassing in his bedroom was utter humiliation. "I'm sorry," she mumbled in apology. "My dog wandered in here; I'm trying to retrieve him."

His smoke-gray eyes regarded her with amused incredulity. "Your dog is under my bed?" He laughed softly.

As if to own up to his crime, Snuffy thrust his head out. The broad spread draped over the top of his fuzzy head as he held the sweater in his jaws, like a trophy.

The hollow feeling in the pit of Hilary's stomach returned. She scooped up the sweater. In the tangle of shredded yarn she saw the label and small crest that indicated the costliness of the garment. Inwardly she groaned at the thought of how much of her paycheck it would take to replace the sweater.

"I'm so sorry! He just got away from me."

The man glanced past her and shrugged.

"It seems my door wasn't completely shut and your dog took advantage of the situation," he remarked. "But then," he added with a sardonic half-smile, "this is my home and I wasn't aware of any canine visitors."

His home! As she met his insolent gaze, Hilary felt as if her dignity were as tattered as the sweater. Trying to keep her voice calm, she said, "I accept responsibility for Snuffy's misbehavior. I'll pay for your sweater. I'll get you another one."

Laughter bubbled in the man's throat as he took the sweater from her cold fingers and held it up in one hand.

It was no longer a sweater, but a mass of string. The owner grinned and looked at her. "He's Snuffy; you're . . . ?"

"I'm Hilary O'Brien." She gulped.

"Hello, Hilary O'Brien," he stated as casually as if they'd met at a party and not in his bedroom while he was almost nude. "I'm Tath Justin."

Her worst fears were confirmed. She felt another flash of anger at Snuffy. "I was afraid of that," she murmured to her new employer. "I'm sorry, Mr.—"

"Tath," he interrupted emphatically. She wished his gaze were not so disturbingly intimate.

"I'll have Snuffy out of here right away," she promised. "He's going to a kennel." Anything, she thought, to get the terrier out of this house. She longed to escape Tath Justin's familiar scrutiny herself. This was hardly how she had envisioned her first meeting with the newest client of Visual Communications.

Tath glanced at the dog. After dropping his shredded sweater on the bed and placing the bottle of after-shave on a bedside table, he scooped up Snuffy. The moment he did, Snuffy reached up and tried to lick Tath's firm chin.

"Are you staying here?" Tath asked her, tickling the dog's neck affectionately.

Hilary was more confused than ever. "Of course. I—"

Before she could explain that Elliot Compton had told her she was to stay at the Justins' home, presumably at their request, Tath interrupted. "Look, there's room for Snuffy here. He doesn't need to go to a kennel, because there's a dog run in the backyard. My father had it built when I was a kid. We had a collie briefly—he was run over by a car only a few months after we got him." He extended his hand. "Come here and I'll show you the dog run—"

Blunt, tanned fingers closed lightly around her arm and he led her to the window. With Snuffy tucked under one arm, Tath stood almost touching her. She was nearly overcome with vertigo. Was it merely her imagination, or did Tath, too, feel the same visceral connection between them? She had never felt so deeply attracted to a man—or so inexplicably afraid.

Carrying the sweet aroma of lilacs, a cool breeze blew through the open window, but Hilary was far more conscious of the barely clothed, virile body only inches away, and of his fresh scents of after-shave, a touch of musk, and soap. When he released her to point to the dog run outside, she noticed dark hairs covering the tanned, muscular forearm. Although he was the head of Justin Mills, it was obvious this man didn't spend all his days sitting behind a desk in an office.

"You can keep him there where you can get him when you want," he said.

Across a backyard filled with oaks, blooming azaleas, and weigela bushes, beside clumps of white spirea, was a fenced concrete area shaded by an elm. Inside the fence was a white wooden doghouse.

"That will be fine. Now about the sweater. If you'll tell me your size..." She turned to look up. Her voice faded as he faced her and his smoldering eyes drank deeply of hers. Suddenly the walls seemed to converge and the room was overpowered by this utterly sensuous man with coppery skin and muscular chest covered by a mat of dark hair—this man whose expression indicated amusement at her predicament, and also something much more disquieting.

His voice husky, he said, "Have dinner with me tonight, Hilary O'Brien, and we'll discuss my size."

The invitation caught her by surprise. She hardly knew what to answer. "I feel so terrible about this..." she began lamely.

"Eight o'clock?"

"There's no need for that, really." She glanced at Snuffy. "At the moment, I wish I'd never picked him up. Two weeks ago I found him abandoned on a highway. He was starving and weak, so I took him home. Now he doesn't want me out of his sight."

"I don't blame him for that," Tath Justin said with unmistakable innuendo.

She attempted a smile, feeling she should take Snuffy, yet not wanting to reach for him. Tath held the dog as a quarterback might hold a football, tucked under his arm, pressed against his bare side. Hilary wished he'd set the dog on the floor. She suspected Tath knew what was bothering her and that he was enjoying the moment. Snuffy looked angelic, wagging his tail happily.

She shifted slightly. "You've won a friend." She glanced pointedly at her pet.

"I hope I've won *two* friends."

Again she gave him a tentative smile. Mustering her aplomb, she said, "I'll get out of your room."

Tath didn't move a muscle. "I'm rather enjoying the conversation."

"We can continue it tonight." The words escaped her lips before she had a chance to consider how suggestive they might sound.

Tath's eyes were twinkling. "Okay, he's yours," he said

easily, but he made no effort to hand the dog to her. Instead he remained still, watching her.

A ripple of consternation went through her and she met his gaze. His gray eyes held a mocking challenge.

In a low voice studded with irony, he said, "If you'd watched him, he'd never have gotten under my bed..."

She realized he knew she was too embarrassed to reach for the dog, to brush her hands against his bare skin, which she'd have to do if he didn't cooperate and extend Snuffy to her. To her chagrin, as if the terrier were determined to cause her every possible difficulty, he twisted to place his front paws on Tath while he struggled to reach Tath's face.

She had no choice. She extended her arms to take the squirming, wriggling bit of fluff. When she did so, her fingers grazed Tath's smooth, warm flesh as well as her fuzzy dog. Again she felt a thrill of electricity at the brief contact of her skin with Tath's.

Immediately, Snuffy transferred his loyalty and attempted to lick Hilary's chin. Holding him firmly, she started for the door.

"Hilary." Tath's resonant voice stopped her.

She turned as he crossed to the bed to pick up the shredded sweater. He strolled toward her to hand her the mangled garment. "Here. Snuffy might as well enjoy himself."

"He doesn't deserve it."

"Oh, but he does," he replied with an engaging smile. His voice deepened. "I'd give up a sweater any day to meet you."

Suddenly, the ridiculousness of the situation struck her. Shaking her red hair away from her face, she lifted her chin. "I think that warrants a thank-you." She returned his smile. "At least you're not waving your fist and yelling at me over it."

He raised an eyebrow and laughed. "Hardly." He reached out to touch her chin lightly, then rested his hand on her shoulder. She hoped he couldn't feel the tremor that coursed through her. "No, what I'd like to do to you is far from yelling or waving my fist."

The sensual tone of his voice sent another quiver of

excitement through her. With what she hoped was a nonchalant air, she answered, "I don't think I care to pursue the subject." Even though it seemed a poor time to discuss business, she said, "I'm looking forward to the commercials for Justin Mills."

He looked puzzled for a moment. She thought he was about to ask her a question, but then he seemed to change his mind. "We'll talk about it tonight," was all he said as he followed her to the door. "I'll meet you downstairs at seven. We'll go out; we're not eating here."

Hoping she looked more composed than she felt, she paused to look at him. "Fine, seven o'clock. I'll lock up the menace now."

He laughed softly and she turned to go. Her shoulder blades tingled and she wondered if he still stood in the door of his room watching her, or if he had gone inside. Fighting the temptation to look back and see, she descended the stairs. As soon as she reached the dog pen, she set Snuffy down and gave him a baleful look.

"Oh, Snuffy, how could you! Of all times for you to wander away!"

While he wagged his tail, she dropped the remains of the sweater and picked up an empty bowl to get water from a nearby faucet. When she returned, she clamped her lips together, aggravated at Snuffy's complete disregard of the tangled mass of yarn.

"Ah, Miss O'Brien!"

She turned to see Elliot Compton crossing the lawn toward her. As he approached, she stepped out of the pen and closed the gate.

Dressed in a gray-and-blue suit, the white-haired man who had been her liaison with the Justin family strolled in her direction. While she watched him, Hilary thought about the arrangements she had made with him, including her two weeks' stay at the Justins' home. The comptroller had even encouraged her to bring Snuffy along. She'd met Elliot Compton the second day after she found Snuffy abandoned beside a highway. The dog had been barely alive and she had improvised a bed in her office where she could care for him. When the congenial Mr. Compton had looked inquiringly from Snuffy's makeshift home to her, Hilary found herself telling him the story.

"Naturally, you won't want to leave your new pet with a stranger while you're at the Justins," the comptroller said sympathetically. "So by all means bring him with you. Tath Justin's quite a dog lover himself, and Snuffy's attachment to you will get you two off on the right foot," he had assured her.

"Tath Justin? I understood that since Mr. Robert Justin's death eight months ago, his widow and two sons are running the mills as a triumvirate, Mr. Compton," Hilary had said.

"Call me Elliot," the jovial, white-haired man told her with a grin. "And yes, that's correct, Bob left the mills to all three of his surviving family members. But the commercials are Tath's special project. He's the younger son, but in my opinion he has a better head for business than his brother Greg."

"I see," Hilary said briskly. She didn't want to become involved in any infighting that might be going on within the Justin empire. "You don't think the Justins would consider it an imposition—not to mention unprofessional—if I brought Snuffy with me to their home?"

"Not at all," Elliot had replied easily.

But of course the comptroller could not have foreseen the havoc Snuffy had wreaked on Tath Justin's expensive sweater, Hilary thought now as she and Elliot met on the lawn.

"Hello, Hilary," he said pleasantly. "Are you and Snuffy all settled in?"

"I guess you could say that," she replied dryly. At his bemused look, she explained, "Snuffy got away from me. He went to Tath Justin's room and tore up one of his sweaters."

"Oh, my word!" Elliott Compton exclaimed. "When I encouraged you to bring Snuffy here, I didn't dream the dog would get one of Tath's sweaters. But don't worry about it." As if to underscore his own lack of concern, he erupted in a burst of laughter.

"Don't worry about it! At the least, I'll owe him a new blue sweater."

Elliot shrugged. "If it comes to that, I'll pay for the damage. But surely Tath bears no grudge—believe me, one sweater more or less will make no difference to him. In fact," he assured her, "the whole incident was probably a blessing in disguise. Got you and Tath acquainted right away and on a light note, eh?"

"He did seem more amused than angry," Hilary admitted. Despite Elliot Compton's avuncular manner toward her, she was hardly about to tell him all that had transpired between Tath Justin and herself.

"Splendid, splendid," Elliot said heartily, with an enthusiasm that rather baffled Hilary. "Tath's certainly never lacked for a sense of humor." He hesitated. "And, er, did you discuss the commercials with him, by chance?"

"Not exactly. We're having dinner together tonight, and we'll discuss them then."

"Now that is really splendid!" Elliot said gleefully, his usual dignity deserting him for the moment. Hilary was more puzzled than ever. In agreeing to do the Justin Mills commercials, she had thought she was merely taking on a new and challenging professional assignment. She had wondered slightly at being expected to reside at the client's home for the duration of the assignment, but Elliot had evaded her questions glibly, and she had chalked it up to some idiosyncrasy on Justin's part. Now she wondered if there wasn't more to this job than met the eye; Justin Tath hadn't exactly acted like a prospective employer, and even Elliot seemed to be personalizing the whole situation.

"Come on, I'll give you a tour of the house," he said before she could hint at her growing doubts.

Behind them a series of yips drowned out melodic birdcalls. Forgetting her misgivings, Hilary turned to glance at Snuffy.

"Since I found him and took him in, he doesn't want me to leave him," she explained to Elliot.

"Bring him along while we look at the house."

"Oh, no. He'll be all right in a minute. Right now I'd gladly give him away."

"Don't worry about the sweater," Elliot said dismissively.

She felt a twinge of annoyance; she didn't like his cavalier attitude toward Tath's damaged sweater, but she felt helpless to combat it. While Elliot Compton waited, she stood still and said, "I do wish you'd explain about Snuffy. I mean, I don't want Mr. Justin to think I'm some kind of eccentric who brings my dog along every time I go on a business trip."

He laughed. "Oh, I'll tell him I egged you on, all right! Don't worry about that. We'll have a good laugh about it."

Her irritation began to rise. "I didn't have a good laugh over it; it was embarrassing."

"Come along now, Hilary. And stop worrying about the sweater. I told you—Tath can afford it. And he loves dogs—felt the loss of his own very much."

"The collie? Yes, he mentioned that."

"Did he?" Again Elliot seemed delighted. "Tath is really an unusually sensitive person. As you'll discover. But I promised you a tour of the house." He motioned to her and started toward the Justin residence. Hilary sighed and moved with him.

They crossed a spacious lawn filled with tall, greening oaks, shorter white dogwood, and pink flowering plum trees. Beneath the trees, in masses of pink, red, and lavender, were clumps of weigela and azaleas.

Soft grass silenced their footsteps, and the only sounds were birds; nearby, Hilary noticed a blue jay splashing in a birdbath. The elegant mansion reminded her of Blake Crowley's home. Even though this was a Southern mansion and the Crowley home was far to the north in Boston, both represented the same thing—wealth and a long line of aristocratic ancestors. She thought of her dark-haired ex-fiancé, remembering the first time he'd shown his home to her. At the time, the house had overwhelmed her; during that first visit she'd felt that it was impossible for the man who lived in it to love her. Wryly, with hindsight and a touch of pain, she realized her first intuitions had proven correct. Blake Crowley wasn't destined to marry any women other than one of his own background. Abruptly she brought her thoughts back to the man beside her; she knew the dangers that lay in thinking about Blake.

As they paused in the doorway of a solarium filled with white wicker furniture, lime-colored cushions, and a multitude of plants, Elliot said, "Madeline Justin redecorated this room before she left for Europe. Since she's away, most of the staff is temporarily gone, but the house won't be so empty tomorrow. It's the second Tuesday in April, and she'll be home."

"Do both brothers live here?"

"No. Actually, neither one does. Tath's staying because he's bought a houseboat and it won't be ready for him until tomorrow or the next day."

"Are you here often?"

He smiled. "I help Madeline with financial matters, so, yes, I am."

From the moment in her office in Dallas when Elliot had first proposed the trip, it had seemed odd to Hilary that the Justins would insist she stay at their home for this assignment. Her doubts intensified as she let Elliot guide her through the mansion. The Justin residence looked like the last place where one would conduct business. It made Hilary think of movies of beautiful women with sweeping gowns and men in Confederate uniforms. Suddenly she decided to confront Elliot with her reservations.

Turning to look at him, she asked, "Wouldn't it be better if I stayed at a motel? I don't see any necessity . . ."

Gazing at her with wide eyes, he smiled. "My dear, these commercials are Tath's project. The mill is so much a part of his life that I feel you should become familiar with his methods. This is a large house; it will accommodate you."

Elliot Compton looked harmless, yet she had a feeling there might be more to this job than he'd indicated. His pink cheeks, blue eyes, and white hair made him a perfect candidate for a department-store Santa, she thought, but when she remembered his fit of laughter over her predicament with Snuffy, she suspected he was more complex than she'd originally thought. Indeed, she was beginning to feel out of her depth with the entire Justin entourage.

Yet she checked further objections. If they wanted her at the Justin house, that's where she'd stay. As she and Elliot strolled from room to room, the comptroller introduced her to a gray-haired maid, Lena, and the cook, Beatrice. Finally, in the center of the main hall, Elliot turned to face her.

"I have some errands to run. You said you're having dinner with Tath, so I'll see you tomorrow."

Nodding agreement, she followed him to the door and closed it behind him. It seemed odd to stand in the doorway of the mansion, to see Elliot Compton out, and to go inside as if it were her home.

Shrugging away uneasiness, she went to her car to get a box of dog food she'd brought for Snuffy. After she fed him, she played with him for a while before going to her room to finish unpacking. At the head of the stairs, she glanced at Tath's closed door and remembered their encounter—the sensuous warmth in his voice and the gleam in those gray eyes. She could be sure of one thing: Tath Justin was no ordinary, run-of-the-mill client. With trepidation she entered her room and drew a bath, hoping a leisurely soak in the tub would relax the tension that pervaded her body at the thought of her dinner engagement with him.

- 2 -

A FEW MINUTES before seven, Hilary started downstairs. Tath was waiting for her in the hall at the bottom of the staircase. His appraisal took in every inch of the immaculate white piqué dress that was her own creation. His gray eyes lowered to study her long, tanned legs and high-heeled white sandals before rising with the same deliberation to her coppery hair, which curled above her shoulders. As she smiled, Hilary felt ten degrees warmer. The dazzling smile he flashed her in return only increased her confusion.

His rugged handsomeness was heightened by a dark blue blazer and a white shirt above charcoal-colored slacks. For an instant she speculated about working closely with this man for the next two weeks.

As she approached, he looked amused. "I don't think I'll make even one complaint to Mother," he said with a cynical note to his voice.

Hilary frowned. "What do you mean?" She couldn't imagine what his mother had to do with the commercials. Elliot had said they were Tath's own special project.

Taking her arm, he grinned down at her. "She made a good selection."

Hilary wondered if the choice of Visual Communications had actually been his mother's decision. All this time she'd thought it was Elliot Compton's and Tath's. She remembered how much Blake's mother influenced his life, made decisions for him—perhaps Tath Justin's was the same. She started to ask about it, but they stepped outside.

While a cool gust of wind struck them, thunder rumbled faintly in the distance. As Tath held the door to a black Porsche, he gazed at the gathering clouds and frowned. When she climbed inside, Hilary thought of Blake's black

15

Ferrari. There were vast physical differences between Tath and her former fiancé, but the commanding air of self-assurance of men born into wealth was the same.

Once they were on the street, Tath glanced at her and asked, "Where do you live?"

"Dallas," she replied.

After removing a pack of cigarettes from an inner jacket pocket, he offered one to her. When Hilary declined it, he lit the cigarette himself as he looked at her thoughtfully. "Dallas . . . O'Brien—is your father Taylor O'Brien?"

She shook her head and smiled. "No. You don't know my father or any of my other relations. And you and I have never met before today."

He quirked an eyebrow at her. "How can you be so certain?"

"I wouldn't have forgotten," she stated, realizing too late how it sounded.

He laughed softly and cracked the window to exhale a stream of smoke. "That's not a Dallas accent. It sounds more like Chicago."

"That's right. Chicago, St. Louis, Boston, Des Moines, Dallas—I attended eight high schools."

Curiosity showed in his eyes. "Where on earth did you meet Mother?"

"I haven't met your mother yet."

His eyebrows rose. "You're not a guest of Mother's?"

"No." They were back to his mother again. This time Hilary asked, "What does your mother have to do with the commercials?"

He frowned and, ignoring her question, asked another of his own. "Whose guest are you?"

She twisted in the seat to stare at him. "I thought I was *your* guest."

The look he gave her sent a wave of heat coursing through her. She added hurriedly, "I mean, I thought it was your idea, your arrangement that I stay at your house for the duration of the project." She wondered what was the matter with her; he had her stammering like a schoolgirl.

Suddenly his eyes narrowed and he shook his head a

fraction. "Elliot! Did Elliot invite you to stay at our house?"

"Yes," she answered. She was startled by his questions and his reactions. "I thought he was acting on your instructions."

"I really didn't think Elliot would..." His voice trailed off and he glanced at her. "Have you been to New Orleans before?"

When she shook her head, he changed lanes and turned a corner. "We'll drive down Bourbon Street. You'll have to see the French Quarter."

Perplexed, she studied him. This whole situation was becoming curiouser and curiouser. "You didn't think Elliot would *what?*" she persisted doggedly.

He glanced at her and smiled. "Go that far. Oh, never mind. Forget it, Hilary." He slowed the car to inch along in bumper-to-bumper traffic as they joined a line of tourists in the French Quarter. "Here's the Vieux Carré," he said, and Hilary forgot her questions about the company as she took in their picturesque surroundings.

Doors to clubs were open, and barkers stood in front, hawking their establishments. Adding to the noise, drumbeats and high trumpets of Dixieland jazz floated in the air from the dark interiors.

Passing small cafés, they reached the corner of Bourbon and St. Ann, where jazz improvisations mingled with the sounds of car motors. As Tath drove toward the river, Hilary looked at the small hotels and restaurants along their route. The stucco buildings were of various pastel colors, some peach, others pale blue or green, all of them decorated with wrought-iron railings along quaint balconies. From time to time, Tath related anecdotes about one building or another, and Hilary marveled at his wit and urbanity.

A throng of people paraded in front of the buildings. With their cameras, brochures, and maps, tourists streamed in and out of the open doors. Hilary noticed a man dressed in a flowing black cape with his face covered in blackface and a wide-brimmed black hat on his head. She pointed him out to Tath, who glanced in the man's direction and smiled. "Probably one of the characters who lives around here.

You'll see everything in the French Quarter."

Within minutes they reached Jackson Square, with its imposing statue of the general and U.S. President. Opposite the square, Hilary gazed at the levee and the Mississippi River beyond it. She said, "Didn't General Jackson save the town from the British in the Battle of New Orleans?"

Tath nodded. "He did more than that. That battle united this country by pulling many different groups of people together. Smugglers and pirates joined the soldiers."

As he turned the car, she spotted St. Louis Cathedral. In the last light of day, its walls were soft yellow. She thought about the history that had taken place before it: the countries—France, Spain, the United States—that had governed New Orleans during the time the landmark church had stood on the site.

Behind the cathedral was a small park walled in by a heavy wrought-iron fence. The spreading limbs of large oaks cast cool, inviting shadows beneath their branches.

Tath motioned with his hand. "To the left of the cathedral is the Cabildo, the Spanish governing building. Between the park and the Cabildo is a narrow street called Pirate's Alley. That's where you'll find the artists now. We can't get any closer by car, because that area in front of the cathedral is blocked off."

Before they left the Quarter, Tath drove past a low-roofed, crumbling yellow building. "That's supposed to be the pirate Jean Lafitte's blacksmith shop," he said. "This is a colorful city built by smugglers, pirates, sugar cane and cotton planters. It's been heavily influenced by both Spanish and French culture, but predominantly French."

Hilary agreed that the French Quarter was fascinating, and she promised herself a longer look at it before she returned to Texas. The old buildings with their walls of soft, muted tints looked graceful. Everywhere were columns and balustrades of ornate wrought iron.

From a sidewalk café came the tempting aroma of hot coffee, reminding Hilary that hours had passed since she had stopped for lunch on the highway into New Orleans. Suddenly she was ravenously hungry.

The car gained speed as they drove from the center of the city to an elegant French restaurant, Chez Jacques, which was hidden from the highway by oaks draped with Spanish moss. Tath left the car with an attendant before taking Hilary's arm to guide her along a canopied walk. As she strolled beside him, a feeling of pleasant anticipation filled her. So far the evening had been thoroughly enjoyable. Tath was a charming and knowledgeable man, and she was looking forward to working with him. Nevertheless, in the back of her thoughts rose a small warning to keep up her guard. If she kept aloof from this good-looking, charismatic man, she'd be far safer; that was what she should have done with Blake Crowley.

When they stepped into the restaurant's dimly lit lobby, enticing aromas of fish and hot bread assailed them. The maître d' greeted Tath warmly and led them across dark blue carpeting to a table decorated with pink carnations and a large white candle. After holding her chair and then seating himself across from her, Tath ordered a bottle of chilled, dry white wine called Les Demoiselles, and fish dinners of truite meunière amandine. Relaxing, Hilary sat back to admire the restaurant's elegant appointments—deep, blue-cushioned chairs and drapes, dark paneling, and antique chandeliers. An assortment of lush potted plants enhanced the decor. In a far corner, a man played a piano softly. She thought about their brief tour of the French Quarter and remarked to Tath, "This is a fascinating city. Has your family always lived here?"

"My ancestors came in 1802, before statehood and even before the Louisiana Purchase, when the United States acquired the territory from France. Nigel Throckmorton Whitney Justin made his fortune planting sugar cane, and added cotton later." He grinned. "Thank goodness I didn't inherit his long name."

She laughed and remarked, "In 1802, my forebears were farming in Ireland." She sat quietly as the waiter reappeared to uncork a bottle, get Tath's approval, and pour their drinks.

Hilary watched as the flickering candlelight cast shadows beneath Tath's prominent cheekbones, giving his dark good looks a faintly sinister air, as if he were one of the pirates or smugglers he had joked about earlier. She reminded herself again to be cautious, to keep their relationship strictly professional. Before she'd left Dallas, her brother Hank had warned her about the Justin brothers; according to Hank, Tath was a notorious bachelor playboy, and his brother, Greg, had four ex-wives.

With an intimate smile, Tath raised his wineglass in a toast. "Here's to a shredded sweater."

Hilary, too, lifted her glass and murmured, "Please don't mention that. I'll get you another sweater."

"It's April. I don't need it." He drank and placed his glass on the table. "You look lovely. That's a beautiful dress."

"Thank you." She smiled. "I made it."

His smoky eyes widened and he studied her. "You're good with a needle. It isn't Justin cotton, is it?"

She shrugged. "I'm sorry, I don't know."

His eyes were dancing. "I bet you can cook, too."

"I can, but I enjoy sewing more."

He gazed at her intently. "Hilary, I'm really curious. How did Elliot talk you into staying at our house? What did he say?"

Her uneasiness returned, but she answered levelly. "He said I should get to know you."

Laughter caused crinkles to appear at the corners of his eyes and creases to bracket his mouth. Hilary did not understand the cause of his mirth, and her confusion deepened when he reached across the table to take her hand and hold it lightly in his. His other hand trailed seductively over hers while he murmured, "You have such slender fingers. Very nice."

The touch of his fingertips raised goosebumps on her arms. Willing herself not to shiver, she looked down at his clean nails, blunt fingers, and wide knuckles.

His eyes took on a suggestive glint. Barely speaking above the sound of the piano, he said, "So you've moved in to get to know me. Well, I'll help every way I can, honey."

The words stung her like a slap. As if his hand were a monster's paw, Hilary jerked her own hand away. Hank had been right about Tath Justin. A wave of anger swept over her—anger at Tath for his insolence, and at herself for relaxing her guard to the extent that he would dare to act so outrageously toward her.

As she conspicuously placed her hands in her lap, Tath looked at her in surprise. "I thought you'd like me to hold your hand," he said in a wounded tone.

"You thought wrong, then," Hilary said curtly.

He settled back in his chair and raised his eyebrows. "You know, you're a little unpredictable. Where did you meet Elliot?"

It was her turn to be startled. "You don't know? I'm from Visual Communications in Dallas." Wondering who on earth he'd thought she was, she added, "I'm here to do the commercials."

Abruptly his body tensed. His eyes narrowed. "Hilary O'Brien." He pronounced her name as if it were the first time he'd ever heard it. His gray eyes frosted and he gazed at her coldly. In a low voice he said, "Oh, no."

Amazed at his reaction, she asked, "What's going on here? Didn't Elliot Compton hire me on your behalf? Didn't he represent you?"

He ignored her questions and his voice grew firmer. "I've talked with Hank O'Brien . . ."

"That's my brother," she stated, mystified at the change in his manner.

"That damned Elliot! Oh, no, Miss O'Brien. I'm sorry, but I hired *Hank* O'Brien."

Her surprise began to change to consternation. "*I* was hired, very specifically—Mr. Compton even had an argument with Hank about it."

"I bet he did! Doesn't your brother own the company?"

"Yes, but I'm production assistant, and Mr. Compton requested me for this project."

His expression denied every word. "Production assistant," he repeated, with emphasis on "assistant." Before he could say more, the waiter appeared, carrying bowls of

green salad. The moment he was gone, Tath looked at her
with steely eyes. "I hired the production chief, not an assistant. I'm sorry for any misunderstanding, but you're not
doing the Justin commercials."

"Just like that? You're not even going to ask to see
samples of my work or give me any fair, professional kind
of trial?" Fury rose in her throat.

He shook his head and scowled. "You're a very attractive
woman, and I'm sure loads of fun, but if your brother
doesn't take over, the deal is off. Elliot's little matchmaking
schemes aren't going to mess up something this vital and
expensive. Sorry to disappoint you, honey, but Greg's the
marrying brother. Feel free to make a play for him, if you
like, but not on company time."

She was shaking with rage. "Of all the rude, crude,
arrogant, insufferable—" she sputtered. "Who do you think
you are? I don't know what you mean by 'Elliot's little
matchmaking schemes,' but you certainly have an inflated
ego to think I would want to marry you."

Out of the corners of her eyes, she was aware of curious
glances from people at nearby tables, so she tried to lower
her voice as she said, "For your information, I'm not interested in marrying anyone. And you—I wouldn't take you
garnished with watercress!"

He laughed. "Garnished with watercress? Never heard
that one before. But then, I've never heard that a woman
didn't want me before, and at the risk of sounding immodest,
I don't believe you. You know, Red, you're real cute when
you're angry, and if you'll keep in mind that I'm simply
not the marrying kind, I'd have no objection to—uh—
getting to know you better."

"Don't you call me Red—or 'honey,' you male chau-
vinist bastard. And will you get it through that swelled head
of yours that I haven't the least desire to marry you?" she
hissed between clenched teeth.

"Oh, no?" he said cynically. "If the possibility of marriage wasn't part of this deal, why did you agree to stay at
Mother's house?"

"Because Mr. Compton insisted that I stay there. I thought

it was rather strange, but I understood that it was *your* preference."

"Oh, sure!"

His attitude fanned her ire into a blazing rage. "You're changing the issue. You think I can't do this job because I'm a woman. That's exactly why you want Hank, isn't it?"

"I want the man I hired," he answered coolly. "You even brought a dog with you, no doubt the better to endear yourself to me. How professional is that?"

Her face flamed with embarrassment as well as anger. "I brought Snuffy at Elliot Compton's suggestion. You cannot hold *me* responsible for *his* motives." She gazed into unyielding granite eyes. "You have no right to feel offended—*I* do. My professional ability has been insulted and I've been greatly inconvenienced. I made arrangements to be away from the office for the next two weeks."

"You'll have to change your plans. Because there's no way you're going to work for me."

Shocked and angry, she stared at him a moment. She had no desire to be employed by a client for any reason other than professional competence, and she wouldn't want to work for Tath Justin if her daily bread depended on it. Still, he didn't have to humiliate her—and with such emphasis. Her fingers itched to slap his face, but she was determined to exit with dignity.

"Very well, Mr. Justin." She rose and started to go, then turned and leaned toward him so that other people in the restaurant wouldn't hear what she had to say. "My brother will be more than happy to step in and do those commercials. I don't want the job if I wasn't hired for my ability." Her voice lowered. "Let me tell you something, though. My acceptance of this assignment in no way involved complicity in any matchmaking schemes. That is the most egotistical assumption I've ever heard!"

One corner of his mouth curled up in a sardonic grin, and his flinty eyes challenged her. "Well, they do say hell hath no fury like a woman scorned, and I guess you're the proof of that statement. But there's no need to go off in a huff."

She started to turn, but his hand closed around her wrist. "Sit down, honey. You might as well enjoy your dinner."

She looked down at the tanned, blunt fingers around her wrist. She wasn't about to resume her seat as if nothing had happened. He'd mortified her, fired her, insulted her, taken away the largest assignment she'd ever had, and she couldn't ignore what he'd done or sit down to eat as if it weren't of any consequence.

She was dimly aware of the clink of dishes, the piano's soft music, and the low sounds of voices, but they faded from consciousness, crowded out by all-consuming anger at the stubborn, aggravating male holding her wrist.

She spoke with all the restraint she could muster. Each word was pronounced distinctly. "Remove your fingers from my wrist."

Suddenly it was a contest of wills, as if all their arguments boiled down to this one thing—he wanted her to stay and she wanted to go. With eyes like cold slate, he looked up at her and ordered, "Sit down."

Pure rage made her quiver. "Mr. Justin, remove your hand."

"Sit down, Miss O'Brien," he said in a mocking tone. "There's no need to get your Irish up just because I guessed why you're here. And this isn't the only job in the world, you know."

Every word was like kindling thrown on a bonfire. "I'm warning you . . ."

Still holding her wrist, he laughed and tipped his chair backward. His dark blue jacket fell open across an immaculate white shirt. His free hand rested on his thigh. He looked relaxed, amused, and infuriatingly condescending. Without saying a word, he conveyed a smug superiority that added to her choler.

As her wrath grew, he gazed up at her with laughing eyes. "You know, you're as stubborn as a ten-year-old Dutch mule . . ."

A Dutch mule! Stubborn! The conceit of the man! Her ears were filled with a roaring sound that shut out everything else.

"That does it!" She leaned forward and pushed.

Surprise flared in his eyes, but he had tilted backward in his chair and she had the advantage. The shove was sufficient to send him toppling over.

But it was her turn for shock. Her small triumph was diminished because he tighted his grip instead of releasing her. She tried to break free, but she couldn't.

As she came down on top of him, her rage vanished in helplessness. Dishes crashed; something struck her shoulder blade, and she yelped as cold wine spilled over her back. For an instant she was entangled with a lean body, hard muscles, and firm hands. A knee pressed against her leg; a stubbly jaw scraped her cheek. She was aware of the scents of blue cheese salad dressing, wine, and musky after-shave. As she struck a table leg, a sharp pain went through her shoulder.

As swiftly as if she had fallen on a hungry tiger, she pushed away and jumped to her feet, mortified that he'd held her, pulling her down with him. She wanted to vanish, to melt out of existence.

He was on his feet instantly to slip his hand around her waist.

"Say, you're a real little wildcat!" He chuckled.

She was enraged as well as embarrassed. How could he appear so cool, so unruffled! Lettuce lay on his shoulder, and there was a piece in his hair. Wine was spilled on his coat. Even with bits of salad sprinkled over him and blue cheese smeared on his cheek, he acted as if he owned the world. Damn him! Cold, wet wine soaked the back of her dress, causing it to cling to her shoulder blades. Brushing salad greens off her fingers, she was rigid with fury as she said, "You've already fired me, now get your hand off my waist before I deck you again!"

His eyes danced with mirth. "You know what you need to cool that prima donna temper?"

She glared at him. "I wouldn't put any low thing past you."

He chuckled again. "You're the one who started this. You pushed us over, remember?" His arm tightened and he looked at her mouth. "You've asked for this."

Before she could say a word, his mouth had covered hers. At first the pure shock of his action paralyzed her, and then she was engulfed by the scent that was part spicy after-shave, part his own virile essence, and by the delicious, surprising softness and warmth of his lips. Horrified both by his temerity and the involuntary surge of desire she felt as his mouth strained against hers, she pushed against his arms in protest. The hard, bunched muscles beneath the smooth material of his coat sleeves resisted her movements, and his embrace became a viselike grip.

To her horror, his tongue invaded her mouth—and worse, her own mouth ignored her mind's command to repel the plunderer. And then all rational thought deserted her, replaced by wave after wave of delicious, tantalizing sensation. Time and place dissolved—she was conscious only of the sensuousness of the kiss, and of the pinprick of need and desire it aroused at her core.

An eternity later, he released her. With a jolt she returned to reality—to the restaurant, to the realization that she'd made a public spectacle of herself, as a loud wolf whistle pierced her consciousness. Other spectators applauded. Tath was laughing again! "Now, if it's possible, just keep calm and I'll take care of this."

She tried to avoid looking around, because she knew people were staring. She was aware of a blur of faces turned their way and a hush in the restaurant. While a busboy picked up spilled dishes, Tath looked around. A man dressed in a white shirt and dark slacks was moving toward them. When he reached their table, Tath gave the man a familiar grin.

"Jack, let me settle this with you," he said. "Meet the cause of it all—Miss O'Brien." He turned to Hilary and removed a leaf of lettuce from her hair as he said, "Hilary, this is the owner of Chez Jacques, Jack Nalley."

She felt as if she were in a nightmare and wished she could wake up elsewhere. Why wasn't Tath Justin as vexed and embarrassed as she was? How could he laugh off what had just happened? She wanted to get away from him, but was afraid to take a step because she couldn't bear another catastrophic scene with him.

"I'll pay for everything," Tath said.

The dark-haired restaurateur shook his head. "That's all right, Mr. Justin. Don't be concerned. We can get another table for you..."

To Hilary, the thought of remaining in the restaurant was ghastly, yet if Tath didn't want to leave, how could she walk out or even argue about it? Without question, the night ranked as the worst in her life. If only Jack Nalley would quit talking and let them go!

"She won't do it again," Tath remarked, and looked at her. "Will you, Hilary?"

She couldn't believe what he'd said. Pulling the tattered shreds of her dignity together, she drew herself up and answered, "I didn't do that alone."

He grinned and turned back to the restaurateur. "I insist on paying, Jack. The lady's temper just got out of hand."

It was going to again, she thought, if he didn't stop his remarks. She spoke up. "I'm sorry this happened, Mr. Nalley."

"That's quite all right. It's nothing..."

Tath interjected smoothly, "Just figure up the tab, Jack. I'll drop by tomorrow and take care of it."

"Fine. Don't you want another table?"

She held her breath a second, and released it with relief when Tath shook his head. "No, thanks." He looked down at Hilary. "I need to change clothes. I've got blue cheese dressing down my shirt."

Another wave of heat flooded her cheeks. Damn him for rubbing it in! She listened as he said, "I'll see you tomorrow, Jack."

Jack Nalley answered, "Okay. It was"—there was the barest pause—"nice to meet you, Miss O'Brien."

She murmured good-bye and let Tath take her arm while they left. All she wanted was to get out of the restaurant and away from Tath Justin.

- 3 -

WHEN THEY STEPPED OUTSIDE, a cool breeze had sprung up. At the sound of a rumble of thunder, Hilary glanced overhead and noticed that clouds hid the stars. They walked to the parking lot in silence; when they reached the Porsche, Tath opened the door on the passenger side for her with an elaborate flourish. Hilary ignored his chronic grin and wordlessly got into the car. As they drove away, she locked her hands together and stared stonily ahead until his laughter made her turn to stare at him.

She couldn't believe he would find the past half hour comical. "You're crazy!" she muttered.

"I'm crazy!" His chuckle deepened. "You flatten me and send dishes flying in one of the most elegant restaurants in New Orleans, and you tell me I'm crazy!"

"If you'll just take me home, I'll pack and leave," she said with as much dignity as she could manage.

"There's no rush. We'll get some steaks. Everything at Mother's is diet food. She even has the staff on wheat germ, bean sprouts, and cucumber sandwiches."

He produced a cigarette and drove in silence. After a few blocks, he signaled and turned into a grocery store's parking lot. "I'll be right back," he said and left to go into the store.

She watched his long stride until he disappeared behind the supermarket's glass doors. What a catastrophic day and evening! She wanted to get out of the car and never see Tath Justin again. She'd made a mess of everything and she was still furious at his attitude toward her. She thought about what she'd have to do. Even though she had no intention of starting the drive to Dallas until morning, she knew she should call Hank immediately and notify him of the turn of events. Opening her purse, she withdrew a pen and a small pad of paper. She made a notation to call Hank, and another to call Elliot Compton because she wanted a word with the man who was apparently responsible for this whole disaster.

As she slipped the pad and pen back into her purse, a rap sounded at the driver's-side window. She looked up to see Tath struggling with three bags of groceries. As soon as she had reached across to open the door and he deposited the groceries on the back seat, she looked down again to close her purse.

"Hey, now . . . tears?" he asked, and placed his hand lightly on her shoulder.

She raised her eyes to his. "Indeed not," she replied quietly, and saw amusement return to his face.

"I thought I saw you tuck a handkerchief in your purse a minute ago."

She glanced pointedly at his hand on her shoulder while she answered, "I was replacing a note pad with a list of calls I want to make tonight. By the way, I'll pay for half the damages in the restaurant, since the fracas was half my fault."

He moved his hand to start the car. "There's no need for that," he said. As they turned into the street, thunder rumbled and large raindrops hit the car. After they had driven a few more blocks, the downpour increased to sheets of gray sweeping over the car. Tath turned on to a wide thoroughfare where, every few yards, tall street lamps shed yellow circles of light whose reflections shimmered on wet pavement. The eerie quality of the scene only added to Hilary's feeling that the whole evening had somehow been unreal.

The torrential rain forced Tath to slow his speed. His strong hands resting lightly on the steering wheel, he gave a low groan.

"What's wrong?" she asked.

"So far this year, we've had eleven inches above normal rainfall and three of those inches fell in the last few days. New Orleans is a bed of water anyway."

"Will it flood?"

He shook his head. "Not here. If we get too much rain, they'll open the Bonnet Carré Spillway, which diverts flood-waters to Lake Pontchartrain. But our mill is in Chalmette and could be flooded."

"Looks like this is going to be a bad storm," she remarked as another deluge hit them, splashing against the car until the wipers couldn't carry off the water. Tath swore, signaled, and pulled abruptly onto the shoulder.

"We'll wait a minute until it lets up."

"Other people have the same idea," she observed, nodding toward a few cars ahead of them along the shoulder. Opposite them, across the divided four-lane highway, a truck had stopped.

Rain drummed on the car while Tath settled back in his seat. As she looked out the front window, the certainty grew that he was studying her until she couldn't resist turning. With a strangely soft look in his eyes, he said quietly, "I'm sorry to take away this assignment, but I want the man who did those Crown commercials."

His announcement sent a shock through her. Deep within, she felt an explosive flare of satisfaction as she remembered the four commercials she had done for the Crown Oil Company of Dallas. Trying to keep her face impassive, she told Tath, "You're going to have a hard time getting him."

His eyes narrowed. "When I talked with your brother, he seemed happy to have the account."

"He was. Did he tell you he did the Crown commercials?"

"Yes. Last February, when I started looking into this, he flew to New Orleans with a reel of commercials for me to see. Those Crown spots were excellent, and that's why I wanted your company. I'm sure when Elliot saw your pretty face, he got sidetracked."

Inside, she felt a wicked, gleeful satisfaction. It was a hollow triumph, she knew. She had a few words to say to her brother when she got home, but she wasn't surprised that he hadn't given credit to her. A year and a half ago, when she had begun to work for Visual Communications as a scriptwriter, after the stormy broken engagement with Blake, every step of the way seemed like an uphill fight to win Hank's grudging approval. She felt she had two things against her in his eyes—she was a woman and his little sister.

She sat quietly while Tath repeated his earlier remark. "I'm sorry, but this is too big to take any risks, and I need the man who did those commercials."

"Well, unfortunately, you'll never get him."

"You already said that, and I don't understand why."

She delighted in every word, but she made an effort to keep any trace of smugness from her voice. "My brother is as chauvinistic as you, and he's probably too afraid of losing your business to tell you that a man didn't do those Crown commercials."

He looked intently into her eyes. As the seconds passed, the atmosphere between them became charged. When his face flushed, she knew he'd guessed that she'd done the commercials he so admired.

Finally he asked her, "You made those?"

She nodded.

"They were damned good."

"Thank you." It mollified her somewhat to hear him praise her work.

As though mulling over her revelation, he looked at her a moment longer before he lit a cigarette. He lowered his window a little to let smoke drift outside, and asked, "You said you brother owns the business—do you have any more family?"

She nodded. "Another brother, Jake, who is line producer. My father lives in Dallas, too."

"Is he with the company?"

She shook her head. "No, he's a barber. My mother died when I was thirteen." She asked, "Do you have more than one brother?"

"No, unfortunately."

"Why unfortunately?"

He shrugged. "Right now, Mother is less than happy with both of us. I don't want to run Justin Mills, and neither does Greg."

"You don't like the business?"

He stubbed out the cigarette in the car's ashtray. "I don't mind what I'm doing now, but I don't want to be tied down to it. I'm an oceanographer—I want to get out of that office, away from a desk and back to a ship. I love oceanography. Greg doesn't want to be tied down to anything too long, and right now he's interested in oil. He owns a part-interest in a small company. We both want out of running Justin Mills, but we can't agree on when or how."

While he talked, he stretched his arm behind her and lowered his voice to an intimate huskiness that made her forget the drift of his conversation. It was warm and steamy in the car, and suddenly she was aware of his closeness.

He said softly, "You know, that first kiss in the restaurant was too public to really enjoy..."

She shifted to look at him and said tensely, "You certainly gave it a try. I thought you'd never stop!"

He laughed. "You stopped resisting, though."

"I was curious to see how long you'd continue," she lied coolly. He mustn't guess how she had been affected by that kiss!

His voice was low, almost a whisper. "Did your brother work with you on those commercials?"

She could guess what was going through his thoughts. No doubt he couldn't believe she had done such a good job on her own. "No, he didn't," she answered firmly.

He grinned. "Don't get in a huff."

"And don't you get any closer."

He was only inches away; his gray eyes were light, the color of smoke from a bonfire. Fringed with dark, thick lashes, they gazed at her steadily. Her stomach was fluttering with nervousness and something more. She glanced out the window. "I think you can drive safely now."

Without moving, he looked past her for a second before meeting her gaze again. "You're right, I can." His voice was low and amused. "You know, I haven't felt this way since my earliest high school days. You don't want me to kiss you, do you?"

The scent of his after-shave filled her nostrils. The fluttery sensation in her stomach grew more intense. She forced her voice to lightness. "I've tried as politely as possible to convey that message."

He squinted at her slightly and drawled, "Sure you're not trying to get revenge?"

"I'd hardly call withholding my kisses revenge."

"I don't know. That's a woman's standard trick..."

All the anger that had died down was suddenly fanned into life again. She glared at him a moment while she debated rising to his taunt or ignoring it. Suddenly she slipped her arm around his neck.

"All right, Mr. Tath Justin. Just so you'll know that I'm not withholding anything out of pique..." She moved the few inches necessary to place her mouth on his. She wanted to straighten his curly hair with her kiss.

Never before in her life had she kissed a man in deliberate provocation. With her arm around his neck. one hand on his broad shoulder, which was warm through his jacket, and her other hand on his arm, she closed her eyes and put all she could into the kiss.

For a second, he sat still while her tongue boldly explored his mouth; then, in a deft movement, his arm slipped around her waist and he lifted her onto his lap to crush her against him. His response was more than she had bargained for, his answering kiss far more. He shifted so she lay in his arms with her head against his shoulder, her legs curled on the seat of the car while he kissed her in a fiery thrust that probed and explored as fully as her kiss had.

A warm tingling started in her toes; as she slipped her hand across his chest, she felt his pulse race. Dimly she thought she might be the one whose curly hair had straightened. His warm fingers shifted, caressing the back of her neck with feathery movements, sending ripples of heat through her entire being.

As he continued to kiss her, she knew she had started something she shouldn't have, something that had already gotten out of hand. His passionate kisses evoked a desire she didn't want to feel. His strong arms held her tightly while her heart's pounding drowned out all other sounds.

This wasn't what she'd expected when she'd put her arm

around his neck to pull his head closer. She wriggled and placed her hands against his chest, pushing slightly.

Instantly his arms relaxed and he raised his head a bit. "You don't do anything halfway, do you?" he whispered.

A rap on the other side of the steamed glass startled her and made her forget his question. Before she could move, he lowered the window and a policeman peered down at them.

"You folks got a problem?" he asked gruffly.

Hilary's cheeks were suffused with crimson as she scrambled out of Tath's arms and slid to her side of the car.

She could hear the laughter in Tath's voice as he answered easily, "No problem, officer. We just pulled over to get out of the storm."

"Yeah, well, see that sign? It says 'no parking.'"

Tath started the motor. "We're on our way, officer." He signaled and moved into the lane, passing the police car.

He glanced at her and grinned. "That would've been worth a ticket."

"At least you should take back your accusations."

His voice dropped. "Oh, I certainly do! I can see you didn't hold back anything to get revenge. You just find me naturally repulsive. Even when we're *both* garnished with watercress." He took one hand off the steering wheel and quickly plucked a sprig of the offending green from her hair. He twisted it briefly, like a trophy, before tossing it into the ashtray.

Her lips curved into a smile. "No fair. I said that only after extreme provocation."

"You're not the only one suffering from provocation, Hilary," he replied, his voice heavy with innuendo.

Deliberately ignoring the invitation in his remark, she said stiffly, "Perhaps we should go back to 'Miss O'Brien' and 'Mr. Justin.'"

"I don't think there's any going back for us, Hilary," he replied suggestively. "Going forward, however, is another story."

"For the moment, I'd just like to go forward to your nice, dry house," she said tartly. She settled in the seat and realized the streets were in better condition than they had been a short time earlier. The rain had changed to a slight drizzle, enough to keep the wipers moving at a low rate, and the road glistened with the shimmering reflection from taillights and neon signs.

Mentally she was circling something, poking at it as a child would poke a strange object with a stick, curious, yet not wanting a sudden, direct confrontation. Yet deep in her heart, she knew it was Tath's kisses that had unnerved her. Never had she been so shatteringly aroused by a mere kiss. Immediately she tried to shove the memory from mind. Glancing at Tath, she was further unsettled to see his full lips curved into a rakish grin. More than ever, he reminded her of a reckless pirate. For the moment she forgot her disappointment at losing the Justin Mills assignment and thought with relief how glad she would be to return to Dallas the next day.

- 4 -

WHEN THE PORSCHE pulled in beneath the portico of the Justin home, Hilary saw another Porsche, a red one, parked by the door. She reached back to get a bag of groceries. "I can carry one. Tath, you have company; don't let me interfere."

"Don't worry, Gloria isn't staying," he answered lightly, and handed her a door key. "Here, you go in. I'll be right there." He stepped over the red sports car, and Hilary glimpsed a beautiful black-haired woman behind the wheel.

Hastily unlocking the door, Hilary entered the kitchen. Ceiling lights illuminated brown wood, gleaming appliances, and a well-lighted work center.

After setting the groceries on a round oak table in the center of the room, she began to put things away, smiling at Tath's selection of pickled okra, jalapeño peppers, canned artichoke hearts, and enough limes to last a year. Along with the gourmet fare, she found two thick steaks, potatoes, and ingredients for a green salad. Including a pound of watercress! Ruefully she glanced down at herself; her lovely white piqué dress was wet with wine and salad dressing stains and smeared with remains of blue cheese.

A motor roared and then faded in the distance as Tath opened the door and entered, a grocery bag in each arm.

She smiled. "I'm unpacking the things you bought."

He waved his hand. "All the comforts of home." Laying the groceries on the table next to the bag she had brought in, he said, "Why don't you change? I'll take care of the food."

"I want to check Snuffy first and see if he's dry. Is there

37

a newspaper I can put over my head to keep off the rain?"

He reached to turn her around. "Get your clothes changed. I know you're uncomfortable with your dress stained with everything but the kitchen sink. I'll see about Snuffy, put potatoes on to cook, and change my own clothes."

She smiled at him. "Okay, thanks." She left and climbed the stairs to her room. After putting her dress in the sink to soak in cold water, she showered quickly, washed her hair and blew it dry before she dressed in jeans and a moss-green blouse that matched her eyes.

When she returned to the kitchen, Tath was standing at the sink with his back to her. While thunder rumbled and rain continued to drum against the windows, she paused in the doorway. Jeans hugged Tath's trim hips, and a navy-blue short-sleeved shirt was tucked beneath a wide leather belt. She strolled forward as she asked, "Can I help?"

He turned and faced her. "If you'd like, but first, did you bring any dog food?"

"Yes. This afternoon I put it in the closet." She crossed the kitchen and opened the closet door to get the box. Tath dried his hands and took the dog food from her.

"I'll feed him; it's still pouring outside."

"Was Snuffy all right?"

He opened a closet and pulled out a light gray raincoat. Slipping into it, he replied, "He's fine. Dry as a box of powder. I'll be right back."

As soon as he was gone, Hilary moved to the sink, where she found a bowl half-filled with lettuce. She picked up the head to tear off more leaves for salad. In a few minutes, there was a knock at the door.

Wondering if it was Tath, she turned. Before she could call to come in, the door opened and a stunning blonde in a white raincoat entered and folded a scarlet umbrella.

The moment she saw Hilary, she halted. "Where's Tath?"

"He's gone to feed Snuffy," Hilary couldn't resist saying.

The blonde's blue eyes widened, and her voice held a note of disbelief. "Snuffy?"

"That's my dog."

"Tath's out in the rain with a dog?"

While Hilary nodded, the blonde compressed her lips. She said, "You can tell him Meredith came by." Her eyes narrowed and she asked, "You're not another one of his mother's little projects, are you?"

"I don't understand."

"You're not here at his mother's invitation?"

Hilary remembered Tath's same assumption. "No," she stated flatly. "I'm a business associate of the Justins'."

"Oh, really?" The blonde's voice was frosty as she pulled her raincoat tight beneath her chin. "Well, tell Tath I'll talk to him later."

Before she could turn around, the door rattled and Tath swept into the room. He stopped, facing Hilary and Meredith, while water dripped in a puddle around his feet. In his hand were wet flowers—lilacs, spirea, and forsythia— which glistened with drops of rain.

"Hello, Meredith. Have you met Hilary?"

She tilted her head to study him. "You've been out in this rain picking flowers and playing with a dog, Tath? Leaving your, uh, business associate to wash the lettuce leaves?" she added with a disdainful nod toward the sink. Without waiting for his answer, she said, "I think I'm intruding." She headed toward the door. "We'll talk some other time. 'Night, Tath."

Grinning like the Cheshire Cat, Tath held the door and said good night to Meredith. When she was gone, he closed the door and hung up his coat. After rummaging in a cabinet for a vase, he found one and carried it to the sink to fill it with water for the flowers. Hilary leaned one hip against the counter while she watched him.

"Thank you for the bouquet."

He smiled. "Can't have dinner without flowers."

"If you can manage without my help for a moment, I need to use the phone."

He glanced at her. "Sure, go ahead."

She left for the privacy of her room, where she tried to place a call to her brother and discovered that the telephone was out of order. By the time she returned to the kitchen, coffee was perking in an electric pot and Tath was closing the broiler door on two steaks. His rain-spattered bouquet on the oak table brightened the room with a touch of color.

"Your phones are dead."

He glanced at the window. "Probably this storm." As if to emphasize his words, a clap of thunder rattled a windowpane.

While he opened a bottle of Burgundy and poured two glasses to place on the table, she said, "I don't have Elliot Compton's phone number, but before I leave New Orleans in the morning, I'd like to talk to him. He seems to be at the bottom of the misunderstanding about why I came here. Though why he would connive to create such an awkward situation totally eludes me."

"Oh, Elliot likes you," Tath said jovially.

"Does he always humiliate and inconvenience people he likes?" she demanded angrily.

He turned to study her, and placed his hands on his hips. "You really don't know, do you? Elliot and Mother hope to get me married. You are apparently Elliot's handpicked candidate for my bride. That's why he hired you and asked you to stay here."

"I don't believe it!" She remembered Tath's accusations in the restaurant, but it was an impossible idea. "You're a grown man. Why would they interfere like that?"

"They want me married so I'll settle down and run Justin Mills instead of sailing away to the ends of the earth on what Mother calls my 'little expeditions.' If I take over, Elliot can retire, so he's willing to aid Mother in her schemes. They've given up on Greg; he's convinced them he's hopeless. For some reason they're concentrating on me instead."

"How awful!"

His eyes narrowed. "I think so too, but few women have that reaction."

"Your mother and Elliot Compton are a match for my brothers. They married young and think I should, too."

"You really don't want to get married?" he asked in a skeptical tone.

"I'm in no rush," she answered lightly.

"Well, we should get along fine." A sensuous warmth

in his tone put her on guard as he moved closer.

She placed her hands against his chest. "Whoa, Tath. Let's not have any more misunderstandings tonight." Fervently she hoped he had not understood the feelings his kisses had evoked in her.

He smiled and rested his hand on her shoulder. "You know, I don't usually strike out so completely."

"So I've noticed. Women keep sprouting up around here like tulips in the spring."

He laughed. "It's not that bad." His smile faded and he studied her. "You know, I have some second thoughts about the Justin Mills commercials. I'd like to work with you, Hilary."

For an instant she felt a flash of triumph but immediately it was followed by regret and consternation. He was too eager to embrace her, and she suspected the motives for his change of heart. "Thank you, but if I wasn't hired for my ability, I don't care to accept the assignment."

His eyes widened slightly. "I thought you wanted to do the commercials."

"I do, but since that isn't why Elliot Compton hired me, I have no intention of staying for the—" She broke off abruptly as lights from a car in the drive swept past the kitchen window. Hilary turned indignant eyes on Tath. "Another one! You need to pass out numbers and tell them to get in line."

"Why are you staring at me?"

Startled, she straightened and picked up the bowl of salad. "I'm sorry, I didn't realize I was. I just can't imagine all these women..."

He laughed shakily. "Another hole blasted in my ego!"

Outside, a door slammed. Hilary protested ironically, "Oh, no. I suspect your ego's bulletproof. It's just surprising to me how many women will get out in a storm like this to come see you."

The kitchen door opened and a tall blond man dressed in a black raincoat entered.

Hilary gaped at him. He was almost as handsome as Tath, though in a different way. Tath was a dark pirate, the newcomer a Nordic Prince Charming. The stranger met her eyes and quirked his brows flirtatiously. As he crossed the room to take her hand, he glanced at Tath.

"Brother, do introduce us."

"Hilary, meet my older brother Greg. Greg, this is Hilary O'Brien."

"I'm so glad to meet you," he said suavely, while he took her hand between both of his.

She said hello to Greg Justin, withdrew her hand, and decided she wouldn't have guessed the two men were brothers. Tath's swarthy skin and dark brown hair contrasted with Greg's fair coloring just as much as Tath's long, thin nose and prominent cheekbones were different from the broad, flat planes of Greg's face.

"What brings you by, Greg? I can't recall that you've stopped here in months," Tath drawled in a tone that didn't hide his irritation.

"Have you known Tath long?" Greg asked her, ignoring his brother.

Hilary shook her head. "No. I just met him today."

Tath's face darkened as much as his brother's brightened. Greg reached for her hand again. "Welcome to our house," he said with pointed chivalry. He glanced at Tath. "I wondered why you were staying here."

"Greg—" Tath began.

His brother interrupted, "They called me because they couldn't get you. Do you know the phones here don't work?" He glanced at Hilary, then back to Tath. "Or were you just not answering?"

Tath frowned. "The phones are out of order. Why did they call you?"

"We've got an emergency at the mill."

Tath swore. "You took your sweet time to relay that bit of news. What's happened?"

Greg looked at Hilary. "I was too dazzled by our stunning visitor to tell you when I came in."

"Now I know you're related to each other," she said.

"Our vistor? Listen Greg—" Tath began, but his brother cut him off.

"The pumps can't carry off all this water. The National Guard has been called, and they're evacuating the area where the mill is. They expect it to flood badly."

"Damn! I need to get out there." Tath drew a sharp breath. "I'm glad you got around to telling me."

"If it's going to flood, there's nothing you can do to stop it," Greg said philosophically.

"If I have time, there are things I can move. Did they say how long we have?"

"They expect the area to be flooded in from two to four hours," Greg answered.

A blinding flash of lightning illuminated the windows; there was a crack of thunder and the lights flickered and went out.

"Damn it! Two hours!" As the lights came on again, Tath ran his fingers through his hair. "I need to call Roger." He started toward the door. "I'll stop on the way and phone him. Our new equipment is still crated. If we move quickly, we might save it, get it out to higher ground. I want the files out of the office, too."

"You can't go out there," Greg argued. "Do you know how hard it's raining now?"

"I can try."

"And while you're trying, suppose the water rises too high for you to get away? You'd be stranded, you might lose your car. If power lines go down, it could be dangerous. Besides, Tath, we have insurance for the equipment, so why run any risks?"

Tath's eyes darkened. "We don't have enough coverage for a disaster. We can't get it on an old plant in that area, and there's no way to replace my files, so I'm going out myself."

"Well," Greg turned and smiled at Hilary, "I'll stay and have dinner with the lovely lady."

"Like hell you will!" Tath snapped. "You can help me. Take your car and I'll meet you at the plant." Tath yanked on his coat. "Let's go, Greg. Every minute counts."

Greg cast Hilary a winsome look and shrugged. "I'll call you later." He winked at her and headed for the door.

As he left, Tath said, "I'll be back when I can."

"I'd like to help," she offered.

He glanced over his shoulder at her. "Okay. I'll get one of Mother's raincoats." While he opened the closet, Hilary turned off the broiler and oven. She crossed the room as he pulled out a coat and held it for her.

Tath locked the door behind them and they rushed to the Porsche. Lightning flashed, revealing dark limbs of live oaks, a vivid glimpse of pink, purple, and yellow flowers on an expanse of lawn that was dotted with silvery puddles of water. Hilary looked toward the dog pen, but clumps of spirea hid it from view.

As the car raced along the street, she wondered if Tath would get a ticket for speeding. She glanced at him. "Your brother is quite a charmer."

He smiled and answered easily, "That's the usual female reaction to Greg."

Hilary didn't add that Greg's brother was equally or perhaps more magnetic. Instead she said, "I would have guessed he was your younger brother, not older."

Again he glanced at her and grinned. "You think I look older than Greg?"

"No." She thought about it a moment and said, "You take charge and he lets you."

"Someone has to, and it'll never be Greg unless there's a woman involved."

Conversation ended as he whipped into the parking lot of a convenience store. Hilary watched him sprint to the outside phone and place a call. In a moment he returned to the car and started it again.

"I phoned Roger Mason, our foreman," he told her. "He'll get some men and meet me at the mill. I hope I can get most of the equipment out. Actually, there's damned little we can move."

The windshield wipers made a steady clicking while he concentrated on driving. She shifted to study his thin, straight nose and firm chin. She thought of the two beautiful women who had come by to see him, and cautioned herself that he was indeed the playboy her brother had warned her about.

Lightning crackled, illuminating the street and a district of industrial buildings. The streets were inundated with water, and the car bounced over railroad tracks and turned into a parking lot to halt beside a blue Jaguar that Hilary assumed was Greg's. Before them stretched a sprawling building of gray stucco. She looked down the length of the building to the loading docks, which were closed and vacant. The mill had a deserted, eerie look, with its darkened windows.

"Power failure?" Hilary wondered aloud as she gazed at the lightless building.

"Could be. But more likely Greg turned off the electricity when he got here, as a precaution against electrocution. We'll need the flashlight from the glove compartment—can you get it, Hilary?"

As she reached into the glove compartment for the flashlight, bright beams of headlights turned into the lot. "Thank God, here comes Roger," Tath murmured. "It'll be easier to talk to him inside. Do you want to wait here or come in?"

"I'll come with you," Hilary answered, and stepped out of the car. Tath was at her side and she felt his warm fingers close over hers as he took her hand. Splashing through cold puddles, they walked hurriedly to the door and into a wide hallway. A stack of small packing boxes was piled high against a wall. Another blast of cold, wet air struck her as the door opened again and two men entered. The large search lanterns they carried filled the hall with illumination.

Quickly, Tath said, "Hilary, this is Roger Mason, and Ted Warrior." He turned to his employees. "This is Miss O'Brien."

As soon as they'd spoken, Tath said, "Is George coming?"

Roger Mason, a tall, dark-haired man, shook his head. "No, but Hugh is."

"Okay. Will you get the trucks out and back them up to the dock? I'll open the doors. Let's get those three crates of equipment into the hall. If we hurry, we can get them out of here."

Both men nodded and turned to leave. Tath took Hilary's

arm. "Come to the office with me." They started down the hall, their shoes clicking against the tile floor. The building's musty, damp smell reminded Hilary of the odors in the basement of the home her family had in Chicago years earlier.

They turned a corner and moved along another hallway. Hilary hurried beside Tath in the direction of an open door while he shone the flashlight on the green tile floor so they could see where they were going. They entered the cluttered reception area of a large office and found Greg Justin with his feet propped on a desk. Also on the desk was a mammoth emergency searchlight.

Tath's eyebrows narrowed. "What the hell are you doing? Or rather, *not* doing?"

Greg smiled and swung his feet to the floor. "Just waiting for you."

"Roger and Ted are backing trucks up to the dock. I want these files out of here, too."

Greg rose and came around the desk to look down at Hilary. He reached out to gently tug a lock of hair. "Natural curl. The rain makes it tighten, doesn't it?"

"Greg!"

"I'm coming." He moved away but paused in the doorway of the office. "You know, Tath, this seems ridiculous to me. We're insured enough to pay for a loss."

"I think the insurance is inadequate and I'm the one who straightened out these files. Some of these records can't be replaced, and I don't want to lose them or find them floating around the office tomorrow if I can prevent it. Will you start moving things here while I open the doors on the docks?"

With a shrug, Greg crossed the room and pulled a drawer from a file. Wondering what she could do, Hilary glanced around and spotted a small two-drawer cabinet beside a walnut desk. She reached down to pull out the top drawer. Before she could get it out of the cabinet, Tath set down an armload of papers and stepped to her side to grasp her wrist.

He sounded annoyed as he said, "Oh, no! One of you

won't work enough and the other works too much. These are too heavy for you. Don't lift that drawer."

She wasn't going to get into an argument with him again. "What can I do to help?"

He waved his hand. "Anything you can put up higher might help."

She nodded, and Tath left the office with an armload of papers. Hilary picked up a chair and placed it carefully on top of the desk. While Tath and Greg went in and out carrying files, she moved about the office, rearranging whatever she could.

After several trips, Greg returned to the office and paused. "We'd better leave this swamp soon, or we'll be sitting on the roof for the duration of the storm." He jammed his hands into the pockets of his tight blue denims and looked at her.

"You know, if you were my date, Hilary O'Brien, I'd show you a better time than you'll have puttering around a damp mill." His voice dropped and he coaxed, "Come on. Let's leave brother Tath with his project. He's entertaining himself."

She shook her hands and rubbed her cold fingers together. "No, thanks."

"Come on. He's more interested in machinery and filing cabinets."

"Thanks, but no."

"I don't give up easily."

"I suspected that." Aware of his scrutiny, she picked up a wastebasket and placed it on a shelf. Doors were open in the mill, the air was damp, and Hilary's hands were cold. She had just reached for a box of papers when a brilliant flash of lightning seemed to fill the room, followed by a deafening roar of thunder. Hilary clapped her hand to her mouth to stifle a scream.

Greg's voice lowered. "Let me have your hand, Hilary. Your fingers are trembling."

"Not anymore," she answered quickly, and willed the tremor away.

"This is a hell of a way for you to spend an evening," Greg persisted. "Come on, let me take you out of here.

New Orleans is famous for its marvelous French restaurants, you know."

"No, thank you," Hilary said quickly. At the mention of marvelous French restaurants, she thought ruefully of the catastrophe at Chez Jacques.

"Be good to yourself," Greg cajoled. "Be good to me. I'd really like to take you—"

"*I'm* taking Hilary out of here," Tath interrupted tersely from the doorway.

Greg gave his brother an angelic smile. "Let's all go get something to eat and drink, Tath," he suggested calmly. "Hilary looks cold."

"We're getting out of here, all right. I've locked up and the men are gone with the trucks. If we don't get out right now, floodwater will keep us from going."

"Damn, I knew you'd cut it close!" Greg exploded.

"Come on, Hilary," Tath said.

"There are some boxes here we can carry," she replied, but Tath spoke quickly.

"Leave them. Hurry!"

She crossed the room and he took her arm. As soon as they entered the hall, he swore. Hilary gasped when she stepped into water. The beam of the flashlight cast a circle on the floor, which was covered with a sheen of water. Muddy water crept along the corridor, spreading wherever there was an opening. Greg frowned at Tath and grumbled, "If my Jaguar washes away, you're getting me another!"

"Just hurry!" Tath's hand tightened on her arm while he held the light steady in his other hand. As they followed the narrow beam of light, Hilary felt as if she were in a cave. All three of them wore Western boots that splashed noisily with each step through the dark mill.

Hilary drew a sharp breath and Greg glanced at her as he grumbled, "This is what I get for trusting a guy who loves water. You may have a swim in the Mississippi soon, Hilary."

"I can't swim."

Simultaneously, both men echoed her statement. "You can't swim?"

She peered through the darkness at Tath. "No. I've lived in cities away from water..."

"Every city has a public pool," he said.

"Well, I never had time to go to it." Suddenly she was aggravated with them. They'd grown up with luxuries she'd never enjoyed, and she didn't want to be treated like an oddity for it.

As if talking to himself, Tath said, "I don't know anyone younger than Mother who can't swim."

"Well, you do now!" For a moment she forgot the water, the darkened mill, their hollow, echoing footsteps, and the chill, dank air.

Greg looked down at her as he walked at her side opposite Tath. "I'll teach you how to swim." Without waiting for her response, he glanced over her head at his brother. "Where do you want to go for a drink? I'll meet you."

"It doesn't matter," Tath replied. "We'll follow you." While they talked, Hilary watched the circle of light bobbing a few feet ahead of them. Beyond its beam everything was dark, and she was aware that the splashing of their steps was growing louder as the water deepened. They rounded a corner of the hall and she heard running water.

"What the hell is that?" Greg asked.

"Probably water pouring under the door into the mill," Tath answered. He told Hilary, "The machinery is in a large room that's about three steps down from this level."

She hated the dark hallway full of rising black water. She hadn't been in a flood before, and she tried to keep her imagination still.

"I hope we can get out of here," Greg said, and opened the door.

- 5 -

A SEA OF water surrounded the building. Lightning flashed and Hilary had a quick surge of panic at the sight of brown water everywhere. Gone from view were the parking lot, the street, the curbs. Looking incongruous, a chain-link fence rose from the water. Cold rain splashed against her hands and face, causing her to pull the raincoat high beneath her chin while Tath locked the door.

Greg stared at the surrounding floodwaters. "It's still not deep—look at the tires." He glanced at his brother. "Are you going to follow me?"

"Yes. Let's go." Tath straightened while Greg looked down at Hilary and squeezed her hand. "See you in a drier climate!" He dashed through the rain to the blue Jaguar.

Tath turned off the flashlight and jammed it into his pocket, turning in scoop Hilary into his arms.

"Hey!" she protested. "This really isn't necessary."

"I'll be the judge of that," he said, his powerful arms tightening around her. He added, "If you'll put your head on my shoulder, your face won't get wet."

She took his suggestion, and her forehead touched the cold, rain-wet shoulder of his coat, her temple pressed against his warm neck. Her nostrils were filled with his heady, masculine scent, and the contact of their flesh sent a shiver up her spine that had nothing to do with the damp chill. To her vexation, she felt distinct disappointment when Tath reached the car and deposited her on the passenger's side. He sat down hurriedly behind the wheel and turned the key in the ignition.

The motor roared to life and he waited while Greg pulled

out and started slowly toward the street, sending waves of
water rippling away from his tires. Tath eased the Porsche
in the wake of the Jaguar and remarked, "Usually, we both
don't have such poor results with a woman."

"What are you talking about?"

"You." He glanced at her, then looked ahead. "Back
there in the office, I heard him ask you to leave with him,
and I heard your refusal."

"That wouldn't have been polite," she said.

"Oh, Lord."

She glanced at him sharply. "What's wrong with that?"

"I'm not exactly overjoyed to find that you're out with
me only because it's the polite thing to do."

She stared at the dark water swirling around the car.
"Frankly, I've wondered several times this evening why I'm
out with you at all."

She knew he looked at her a moment, but she didn't take
her gaze from the water surrounding them. The rain came
down harder, increasing to a torrent, while ahead the Jaguar's red taillights led the way like beacons.

Tath said, "Hilary, do you go with anyone, I mean are
you serious about a guy right now?"

She looked at him. "No. And I have no desire to be for
the moment," she added pointedly. Hastily changing the
subject, she said, "How can you find the street or stay on
it?"

"It must take Mr. Perfect to qualify."

She looked at him and wondered what he was talking
about until she remembered his question. "Hardly," she
answered. "Just a nice, ordinary guy."

"I feel like an ogre with two heads." A flash of lightning
gave a silver-white brilliance to everything, and thunder
boomed.

It was difficult to keep her mind on his conversation. "It
really doesn't matter," she remarked. "I'm leaving in the
morning. We don't have compatible personalities anyway."

"We don't, eh?" Unexpectedly he hit the steering wheel
with his fist. "The steaks! I completely forgot them . . ."

"I turned them off," she stated, and watched as he turned

to follow Greg in the street. With a sputter, the motor died. She drew a sharp breath and looked at Tath.

Rain drummed on the car while Tath tried the ignition. The motor finally revved up, and they eased along behind Greg again, moving slowly as the water level began to lower until they were finally on dry paving.

They followed the blue Jaguar along a busy boulevard where Tath increased his speed, staying a short distance behind Greg's car. Without warning, Tath shifted lanes, turned a corner, and headed in another direction, abandoning Greg.

Hilary looked at him. "That wasn't nice."

"True, but I don't care to spend the next hour listening to Greg come on to you. He can do it on his own time, not mine."

Laughing, she settled back in the seat, relieved to be out of the water. She wasn't particularly sorry to lose Greg, either. In a short time, Tath signaled and turned into a parking lot. "I don't know what this is," he said. "It may be a greasy spoon, but I have to eat."

They entered a cozy one-room restaurant. Even though the lights were low, there was a sheen on the cypress planking of the floor. Hilary glanced at walls lined with booths. In the center of the room were tables covered by red-checked cloths and candles. An enticing aroma of gumbo and hot coffee filled the air. In one corner a jukebox played a country-western tune that drowned out the sounds of conversation.

Tath led Hilary to a table and sat facing her. He glanced around, remarking, "Maybe the food's edible—the place seems popular." He picked up a typed menu encased in clear plastic and studied it. "There won't be any wine."

She laughed. "We never seem to get further than a glass of wine before there's some calamity. I'm not sure I should have another glass anyway, because I haven't eaten since midmorning."

He looked around. "Short of the restaurant flooding or bursting into flames, I think we'll finally get to eat. What would you like?"

"I'm not familiar with some of these dishes. You select something."

"You know, it's time you tasted some of New Orleans' specialties," he remarked as a waitress approached to take their order. As soon as she was gone again he looked at Hilary. "Thanks for the help at the mill. Thanks, too, for turning off the steaks, or the old home place would be in flames by now." He regarded her intently. "You're kind of useful to have around, very cool, collected, and logical—unless you're angry. And even then, you're awfully appealing."

His smile was so boyishly engaging she couldn't help returning it. A waitress interrupted the conversation to place a cold beer in front of Tath and an iced cola before Hilary. He sipped the beer, lowered it, and tilted his head to one side.

"So you're not interested in marriage." The doubt in his voice was unmistakable. "Somehow you look far too earnest to take any relationship lightly."

"If you mean sleeping around, that's right," she said bluntly, hoping he would be put off.

He chuckled and leaned forward to touch her cheek. "Who's the man in your life? There's bound to be one."

"I'm here on a business assignment, Tath, and I don't have to account to you for my personal life. I've already told you there's no steady man." She added flippantly, "I'm too young to get married."

The sardonic glint in his eye denied her statement. "How old are you—twenty-four?"

"Twenty-six."

"Well, at least there we agree," he said lightly. "I'm thirty-two and entirely too young to put my neck in a noose."

"My feelings exactly."

His gray eyes studied her with curiosity. His voice dropped to an intimate huskiness. "You're too full of life, Hilary, to convince me you lead a solitary existence."

"I keep busy."

He shook his head. "Uh-huh. Nobody with that color hair"—he leaned forward and lightly touched the corner of her mouth, sending tingles she didn't want to feel coursing through her—"and lips like these, spends all her time alone."

"Believe it or not, I can live without a man!" she stated forcefully. At other tables, heads turned and Tath glanced over his shoulder while he shook with laughter.

"Lower your voice, Hilary, or they'll have the police after me."

She sipped the cola and gazed at him with far more composure than she felt. She could change the subject, discuss the commercials, but she'd lost her enthusiasm for the project. Between her brother's claim to have made her commercials and Tath's rejection of her without consideration of her professional qualifications, she didn't want to pursue the subject. Then, too, why exacerbate her disappointment over losing the assignment?

He shifted and leaned back to regard her intently. "You know, you admitted more than you realized a minute ago. I'm right."

She looked at him blankly and he continued, "Your remark that you can live without a man—in other words, Miss Hilary O'Brien, you won't settle for anything half-hearted. A man has to offer marriage or you're not going to participate."

She hoped her features were passive and hid her consternation at his logical deduction. He was right in his guess that she wouldn't participate in any light relationship without commitment or love.

"If you want to interpret my statement that way—fine. I don't believe in bed-hopping, but I'm also not ready for marriage."

"You would be, though, if the right guy asked you."

She placed her glass on the table and looked directly at him. "You know, Tath, I think you would be, too, if the right woman appeared."

Swiftly he leaned forward until his face was close to hers; his hand slipped behind her neck. "Don't aim those big green eyes at me like that. You're old enough to take care of yourself." His voice lowered and he caressed her neck in a slow, sensual movement. "I'm warning you right now, I'm not going to ask anyone to marry me, ever."

Her heart thudded, but she gazed steadily into his eyes and licked her lips. "I'll file that away," she answered in what she hoped was a cool tone of voice. "You're quite safe from me, Tath Justin. You're not my type." Hilary grasped wildly for any kind of defense. "You're too young."

"Too young! At thirty-two? What do you want, Grandfather Time?"

Thirty-two wasn't too young at all, but his seductive persistence was unnerving. She twisted slightly so her neck eluded his hand. Attempting to sound as haughty as possible, she said, "I prefer men over thirty-five."

Tath hooted derisively. Ignoring his response, as well as the inner voice that accused her of dishonesty, she added, "They have a certain maturity that younger men don't."

Quietly he digested her remark, and Hilary felt she had scored a direct hit. This man was a challenge; if only he weren't so quick-witted!

He smiled enigmatically, picked up his drink, and held it out. "Well, Hilary, I'm too young, and you're too old-fashioned—so here's to what might have been."

She raised her glass and acknowledged the toast. When he lowered his drink, he placed his chin on his hand to look at her with disconcerting admiration.

"What a damned shame," he uttered with such sincerity that she had to laugh.

He grinned and straightened. "I like to see you laugh. Your whole face lights up."

"I think you're at it again," she chided playfully.

He shrugged. "It's ingrained. A beautiful woman appears and I go after her—like the earth turns and the sun rises."

She smiled. "Red hair and freckles are rarely termed beautiful."

Her remark brought his face close to hers. He tilted her chin up to his gaze and studied her intently. "Then the world is full of unseeing clods," he said. "Your hair is glorious, your freckles are endearing . . ."

She laughed and pushed against his chest. "Whoa. Did you know people keep staring at us?"

"They're looking at you."

"That's not so. Now stop."

"I can't. It's impossible; you're driving me wild."

Hilary laughed. "You're incorrigible, Tath!"

"No. I'm dazzled to my socks by a delectable redhead."

Abruptly, Hilary wished she had said she wanted marriage and a family. She suspected she had presented a challenge to which he had risen full force. If he continued pouring on the charm, it was going to be difficult to remain aloof, and for the first time since Blake, a man held an appeal for her that was increasingly more difficult to ignore.

"What are you thinking, Hilary?"

"You notice things too quickly."

"And what else were you thinking?"

She forced lightness into her voice. "That it's been a long time since lunch."

He leaned back. "You really do know how to burst someone's balloon."

"There's a way to avoid that. Balloons should stay away from needles."

"I can't resist," he answered, his gray eyes winsome.

"I bet you can't—indiscriminately and constantly!"

He leaned forward. "That's not so." His voice lowered as he gazed at her. "I'm very discriminating . . ."

She reminded herself that the same disarming sorcery was practiced on a number of women. She was just one of a series of females on whom he exercised his winning ways; she was certain his remarks had as much meaning as the postman's greeting in the morning and that it was time to change the topic of conversation. Interrupting him, she said, "It's still raining."

He looked at her a minute, then shifted his gaze to a dark front window. The large sheet of glass was spattered with raindrops. In wavering silver streaks, rivulets streamed down the pane. Tath frowned. "I'm afraid Justin Mills is going to have a big loss. If the rain would just stop right now, losses would be minimal."

He ceased talking to watch the waitress set before them steaming plates of jambalaya, a tempting casserole of rice and shrimp, as well as baked yams and crisp fried okra. Along with mugs of coffee, a plate of golden cornbread was placed on the table.

While they ate every delicious morsel, loud claps of thunder occasionally drowned out the jukebox. When they had finished and the plates were removed, they lingered over café au lait made with strong chicory coffee.

Tath scraped his chair back, placed one booted foot across his knee, and studied her. "This is the perfect way to spend the evening—a good meal and a ravishing woman."

"Thank you." Why did he persist in getting personal, she wondered. Whatever the reason, she wasn't going to encourage him. She said, "I've read about Justin Mills and know they started in 1886, but how long have you had the building I was in tonight?"

He looked amused, and she guessed he knew why she had changed the conversation. He answered, "That mill was built by my grandfather years ago, when a flood destroyed the old mill."

"In the same location?"

He nodded and remarked dryly, "You'd think people would learn. I don't know why Dad didn't build in another location. That's a terrible site and the building is poorly constructed for this area. Low and flat, it's a few steps down into the main part of the plant, which is where you heard water running, pouring down those steps tonight. I'd like to build a new Justin Mills, and we have the money for it."

"You sound reluctant. What's holding you back?"

His soft eyes rested on her. "If I started that, I'd never get away from here. For three years now I and some fellow scientists have been planning an expedition to the Antarctic. We've won a grant to help finance it, and we'll turn our information over to the Earth Science Foundation when we're through. I don't want to give it up to sit behind a desk in a cotton mill."

He sipped coffee and lowered the cup to ask her, "When you plan commercials, where do you start?"

"I begin by asking the client what he or she wants." She

wondered why he was asking her about it. She knew her voice sounded cool, but he should understand her reluctance to discuss her work after he'd fired her.

"When I decided to use commercials, my idea was to promote the mills," he remarked. "We've grown—both the mill here and our other mill, in Baton Rouge, are larger, and it's time to make Justin cotton a household word."

She remembered the data she'd gathered before she left Dallas. "Your business increased ninety percent in the last quarter of the year and is predicted to make a strong gain in the first half of this year."

He gazed at her steadily. "You did your homework, all right. I know Elliot didn't tell you that."

"No, he didn't. I looked it up."

He studied her silently for a few minutes. She stirred her coffee, swirling the hot liquid in the thick white mug. She looked up as he asked, "Why don't you do the commercials for me?" Before she could answer, he said in a matter-of-fact tone, "Hilary, I'm sorry. I owe you an apology. My reaction to your doing the commercials was totally out of line—unprofessional and unworthy of you—and I'm sorry."

"Apology accepted," she said crisply. Would wonders never cease, she thought.

He leaned forward and trailed his fingertips along her jaw. "Let's do those commercials. We ought to work well together."

For an instant she'd almost changed her feelings about him, had nearly forgiven him because she thought he regretted his hasty judgment. Now she realized the only thing he regretted was her leaving him. His primary interest in her was as his latest playmate, and she guessed her ability was way down on his list of reasons for wanting her to go ahead with the job.

She answered flatly, "No."

He straightened and looked at her. "What do you mean, no?"

"You fired me and now you want to rehire me—but not for the right reasons. Under those circumstances, I won't take the job."

His eyes smoldered dangerously. "You want me to grovel."

"No, I don't. You could apologize all night and it wouldn't matter."

"I want you to do the job because you did those Crown commercials."

"Somehow I find it hard to believe that's your only reason."

He studied her a minute, then relaxed. "Okay, send brother Hank when you get back to Dallas."

She felt both disappointment and relief, but before she could reply he leaned forward and placed his arms on the table. Looking earnest, he said, "You can send your brother, but I don't want you to leave with any doubts about my sincerity. The only reason I'm offering the job to you is that I admire your work. Don't you know I can ask you for a date just as easily if you're not employed by me as I can if you are? Maybe even more easily."

"I suppose."

"Believe me, from the first, I wanted the same person who did the Crown Oil spots. They're excellent."

Her confidence and trust returned. "Thank you."

"I can keep the line drawn between business and pleasure, and I'm not offering to hire you because of your adorable face."

He was silent a moment and she thought over what he'd said. If he was sincere, and really wanted her because of the examples he'd seen of her work, she would like the job. She nodded. "Fine, I'll accept your offer." She hoped she was making the right decision—when those smoky eyes beseeched her, it was difficult to think rationally.

"Ahh." He smiled and reached across to squeeze her hand. "Good!" He straightened and asked, "Are you ready to go?"

When she agreed, he rose and came around the table to hold the raincoat for her. "You'll still need this."

She glanced at the window and saw the rain-streaked glass, but once they were outside, they discovered that the downpour had abated. Now only a light rain was falling.

Wordlessly they walked to the car. With his customary gallantry, Tath opened the door for her before going around to the driver's side.

"Thank you for holding the door for me," she said primly as he reached into his pocket for the ignition key. "You're really spoiling me with all this chivalry."

He smiled. "Worse yet, I might get spoiled with all the kissing we did earlier. A guy could really get addicted to those sensuous lips of yours, you know."

Her heart raced wildly. "If that's the case, perhaps we'd better put you on cold turkey before you start having withdrawal pains."

He shifted to face her and touched her shoulder lightly. "I'm already having them. And addiction doesn't scare me—I like to live recklessly."

She knew he was teasing, and she answered in the same tone. "A few kisses aren't exactly what I'd call reckless." He gazed at her intently, and she realized the words had come out sounding like another challenge. His hand drifted across her back to caress the curve between her neck and shoulder, shifting beneath her raincoat and blouse to touch bare skin. His voice lowered. "What do you call reckless, Hilary?"

She smiled and looked directly into his eyes. "Maybe some depths are better left unplumbed," she said demurely, hoping she was striking the right note.

"Not at all! We oceanographers are lured to depths," he said emphatically, and his arm circled her shoulders to draw her closer as he leaned forward. "Let me show you . . ."

With sensuous deliberation his lips possessed hers, probing and exploring to send a burst of tumultuous longing through her. An arm slipped around her waist and pulled her to his chest. She felt her breasts straining against him, his taut leanness making her distinctly conscious of her womanly softness. His fingertips circled tantalizingly over her kneecap, sending delicious sensations through the flesh beneath her worn jeans.

Touching his arms, she felt the hard, tensed muscles. She slid her hands up across his broad shoulders, then gradually down until her fingers rested on his shirtfront. Beneath her palms, his heart pounded in hammer blows.

Dimly she realized she'd started something again; her light teasing had only provoked him. Now she wished she hadn't acquiesced in their flirtation, because it was more, so much more than she'd expected. Logical thoughts vanished like smoke in a high wind as his fingers deftly unbuttoned her raincoat and lightly stroked the thin fabric of her blouse, bringing her nipples to taut peaks of desire.

She moaned involuntarily and curled an arm around his neck, snuggling against him. It felt so right, so natural. But suddenly she realized how dangerous her reaction was, how complicated her life would become if she got involved with this charismatic man. All the arguments were against it— he was a womanizer, and now her employer, and his aristocratic background was so like Blake's.... She pushed forcefully.

"Tath, please stop," she whispered, and straightened. Her nipples still ached with longing, but her voice was firm.

The teasing laughter was gone from his eyes as he pulled away. He tilted her chin upward and observed her with curiosity. "You really mean that, don't you?"

She nodded. "Yes," she whispered, and thought to herself that she meant it because she knew she should. She followed the prudent course, fighting to ignore the ache at her core, or what his intent gray eyes were doing to her insides right now.

- 6 -

TATH TURNED FROM her and pulled out a cigarette. While lighting it, he said, "I've been warned this would happen."

"What?"

She watched his strong, brown fingers switch on the ignition, crack the window an inch and rest on the steering wheel. He exhaled and answered solemnly, "I've always been told that someday I'd get a dose of my own medicine." He glanced at her and narrowed his eyes against the smoke. "You don't want me to make love to you."

"No," she said, and thought to herself that her answer was no for all the wrong reasons. She wished he didn't cast such a spell on her, that she didn't respond to his kisses and fondling and inwardly long for more.

He regarded her silently, as if completely lost in his own thoughts, until she finally asked him, "Are we going?"

"Hmmm? Oh, sure." He put the car in gear and backed in a semicircle to drive out of the lot. As he did so, he turned on the radio, explaining, "I'd like to get a weather report and any other news of the flood. I think I'll drive to Chalmette and see if I can find any National Guardsmen in the area where the mill is. Do you mind?"

"No." She settled in the seat and rode in silence while they listened to a news commentator relate facts about the flood and weather. With each flash of lightning, static crackled, drowning out the voice on the radio. They drove past small wooden houses and wound through a maze of streets until they reached an industrial area.

From curb to curb, water flowed, gradually deepening. At one intersection, just as Tath sped across it, she glanced down the street and saw flashing red lights, people milling around, and spotlights illuminating dark water.

He took in the scene at the same time, braked, and turned to drive toward the gathering. At one side of an inundated street were a National Guard truck and a police car. Beyond them, the water rose high enough to flow into the surrounding small frame houses.

"I'll be right back," Tath said, and parked the Porsche. She waited while he stepped out and joined a cluster of men beside the truck.

Looking grim, he returned to the car again and headed out in the direction from which they'd come.

"Bad news?" she asked.

He nodded. "The mill should be under a foot of water now."

"That's terrible! Are you going to try to go there again?"

"No, it's useless now—we did all we could earlier. We're going home."

She settled in the seat to ride quietly for several blocks. Tath pointed out a modern building, and after a brief discussion about its design, she thought about her assignment and asked him, "What did you have in mind for your television commercials?"

He glanced at her and shrugged. "I want to put the Justin name before more people, to increase public confidence in the fact that fabric from a Justin mill is made of fine cotton. The natural fibers have advantages over synthetic fibers. I want to get across that we have a good, reliable product."

She nodded. "I understand from Elliot that you grow your own cotton."

"That's right."

"We might start there, then. May I take a brief tour of your farm?"

"Why the farm?"

"We might get a good shot of a cotton field to emphasize the natural fiber."

"Mmm—I like the idea. Our fabrics are sold throughout the South and Southwest, but these commercials will be on

Louisiana television only. I'd particularly like to stress that this is a state product."

"If you'll show me around, I'll get a storyboard ready." When he glanced at her, she explained, "A storyboard is a series of panels of sketches showing the action planned in a production."

"I see. You may have explained this to Elliot when he was in Dallas, but I haven't had an opportunity to discuss it with him or go over any of the arrangements he made with your agency."

"It's a production company," she explained. "We're different from an advertising agency in that we're not agents or middlemen. We're involved in the actual production and our business is conducted mostly with free-lance talent. We specialize in production, so we're limited to commercials and training films."

She shifted in the seat to face him, and tucked her legs under her on the seat. "Let me look around the mill and then discuss it with you. Next I'll put something together to present to you. If it looks like what you want, we'll go on to develop the idea. Visual Communications will do the storyboard and a script, and plan a budget for your approval."

He nodded. "If you film inside the mill, I'll have to get new equipment."

"Old machinery won't matter in a commercial."

"Dad always had good relations with the employees, but he resisted change, including replacing the old machines. Our union leaders are fine people, and so far we've managed to work out contracts and avoid strikes."

"Maybe you'd like some of your employees in the commercial," she suggested.

"That's a possibility. Tomorrow I'll take you through the mill. You need to see some more of New Orleans, too. Tonight was only a preview. How about if we go sightseeing together on Wednesday?"

She felt like answering, "Dangerous." Instead she merely smiled and replied, "Fine."

He slowed and turned in the drive to stop under the

portico of his house. When he opened the door for her, she hesitated and said, "I'd better see about Snuffy. He doesn't like to be alone."

Tath took her arm. "Get in the house, out of the rain. I'll see about Snuffy. Last time I checked on him, he was snug as a bug in a rug."

He stepped inside to switch on the lights, and helped Hilary take off her raincoat. After chilly, damp air, the kitchen held a cozy warmth and smelled faintly of broiled steaks. Hilary shrugged off her coat and looked at Tath while he hung it carefully in the closet. "I hope Snuffy's dry," she remarked.

He glanced down at her with an expression close to tenderness. "He is. Any dog that can get into my room can take care of himself."

She gazed up in surprise. "You don't think I deliberately put him in your room, do you?"

He held up his hand and interrupted her with a laugh. "No, but your bringing him to my house is highly suspect."

"I told you—Elliot urged me to bring Snuffy."

"Good old Elliot." He chuckled. "He knows I'm a sucker for dogs since the collie died. And I couldn't help thinking you were in collusion with Elliot—and Mother. They're determined to marry me off. For the last six months, Mother has continually paraded a bevy of young debs beneath my nose. I figured you were one of them."

"Hardly," she stated so sharply that his eyes narrowed. "Have something against debutantes?"

She looked down, momentarily thinking of Blake and Emily Devon—the very proper Boston girl, debutante, Junior League, and member of a family as socially prominent as Blake's. Hilary did have something against debutantes, but she didn't want to admit it. Moreover, Tath's question was unnerving because he was too quick to discern her thoughts. She answered firmly, "No."

He studied her. "Well, something I said irritated you." When she didn't answer, he drawled, "I'll go check on your dog now."

She closed the door behind him and turned to put away

the food they'd left out in their sudden departure before dinner.

In a few minutes the back door burst open and Tath stepped inside. When she looked at him, Hilary's heart seemed to skip a beat.

He stood inside the door, holding a bundle in his arms. She rushed toward him as he opened the closet and pulled out a small braided rug. He knelt and placed the limp, quiet dog on the rug.

With a frown, he said, "I don't know what's happened to Snuffy."

Hilary hurried to kneel beside them. "Snuffy!" She smoothed the animal's fuzzy hair away and saw a dark brown eye open and look sorrowfully at her.

"He was fine before, but when I went out this time, I found him laying in his house, not moving..."

As Tath's words trailed off, Snuffy's tail thumped against the floor. She sat down cross-legged and spoke softly to him. "Snuffy, you poor thing..."

"I'm sorry if he's sick."

Snuffy's head rose and his tail thumped harder. Hilary leaned closer to speak to him, and he rolled over to climb into her lap, getting muddy pawprints on her jeans. She looked up at Tath and spoke dryly. "Don't worry about him."

Tath's eyebrows lifted. "He looks normal now."

Hilary held the squirming, wriggling dog as she said, "He's the biggest ham. He's a fake and he's punishing me for leaving him."

Tath's dark eyebrows arched higher. "You mean he isn't really sick?"

She looked down at Snuffy, who wagged his tail. "What do you think?"

Tath's voice was filled with disbelief. "He was as limp as overdone spaghetti when I picked him up. He didn't move or open his eyes..."

Snuffy put up his paws and tried to lick Hilary's chin.

"I'll be damned!" Tath muttered. "I've been outsmarted by a dog!"

She laughed. "You're not alone—I've felt that way since the night I picked him up." She handed him to Tath. "Here, take him back."

He took the dog and rose to his feet, holding Snuffy up in front of his face. "You're a real so-and-so, you know that?" he rebuked the terrier.

Hilary laughed as Snuffy's front paws beat the air and he struggled to reach Tath's chin. Tath tucked the terrier under his arm and crossed the room to get a handful of paper towels, carefully wiping Snuffy's feet. Hilary rose and asked, "Aren't you taking him outside?"

Tath grinned. "No. This little fellow's earned an evening inside."

"Don't encourage him."

"He can stay in the utility room tonight. I'll give him something old to chew on."

"After what he did this morning, I don't think he should."

He looked at her. "It's my house."

She shrugged. "Okay, but he's my responsibility, and as you can see, he's a very devious dog."

Tath ruffled Snuffy's woolly hair. "Did you hear that, Snuffy?"

Looking first at Tath, then at Hilary, the terrier wagged his tail. Tath said, "I'm soaked and the house feels chilly. I'll build a fire." He carried Snuffy to the utility room. "How about a cup of hot chocolate, Hilary?"

"That sounds tempting, as soon as I change." She looked at the smudges of muddy prints Snuffy had left on her clothes. As she went upstairs and changed to a pale blue chiffon blouse and a clean pair of jeans, she hoped Snuffy would settle down to sleep and not cause any more disturbances.

When she entered the large den, a fire was roaring in the stone fireplace and soft music was playing on a stereo. Tath had changed his clothes and pulled off his boots and sat on a throw rug in front of the fire. Two cups of steaming cocoa were beside him.

"Come here by the fire."

Hilary picked up her cup and sat down on a rust-colored sofa. "Thanks, I'll stay on the sofa."

With a lithe movement, he shifted quickly and suddenly was close to her, sitting on the floor with one arm propped on the sofa. He reached for her hand and clasped warm fingers over hers. With her other hand, she balanced the cup of hot chocolate on her knee.

Regarding her intently, he asked, "Why are you scared of me?"

"I'm not. You're no different from any other man," she stated forcefully, as if trying to convince herself.

"Thanks." His grin broadened.

"I'm sorry. You're . . ."

"I'm what?"

"You're too disturbing," she answered in a matter-of-fact tone while she tried to remove her hand.

His fingers tightened over hers, and he raised her hand to his lips. "Do I have to get permission to do this?"

She shook her head. "No, but I don't think you should do it."

His lips trailed across her knuckles before he turned her hand. His breath was warm against her palm, sending a tremor through her. He looked at her. "Why am I too disturbing? What's wrong with that? Why do you throw up a barrier if I get personal?"

"Tath, I don't care to answer your questions. We have a business arrangement—let's not jeopardize that."

"It's a business arrangement in the morning. Tonight we have a date—I asked you out to dinner, remember?" He planted a moist kiss on her palm, then his lips trailed softly to her wrist. All the time his hooded eyes studied her. She felt his warm breath caress her palm again, sending tingles up her arm. When she tried to withdraw her hand, he held it firmly.

"Why are you so skittish? All I have to do is touch you lightly, and you freeze."

"Are you calling my kiss cold?"

He smiled and watched her. "No. It singed my tonsils, but you keep resisting me."

Not enough, she thought. She knew she should withdraw her hand now, move farther away from him, stop looking at him and noticing the glints in his dark brown hair, the fine texture of his skin, his sensual lips... It was difficult to answer him, and she tried to keep her voice normal as she said, "That's just the way I am, Tath."

He kissed each fingertip with infinite tenderness and she whispered, "Tath, please..."

"Who was he, Hilary?"

"Who?"

"Whoever made you this way."

For an instant she clamped her lips together to refuse an answer, but the velvety insistence of his low voice and her own trembling yearnings caused her to reply, "His name was Blake Crowley."

"Were you very serious about him?" He raised his head briefly and scrutinized her.

She nodded. "Yes," she murmured. "We were engaged."

"Oh?" His eyes were full of questions.

"Please—I'd rather not talk about it," she forestalled him.

He continued to caress her wrist. Her whole body went tense. "You need to get over that," he chided her gently. "One little kiss on the hand starts you quivering, but then you turn to ice."

The words echoed in her mind. He was right, because one kiss, even one little kiss on the hand, did start her trembling—one of Tath's kisses!

She shifted and moved a few feet away, to the corner of the sofa. He looked amused as he watched her silently before he turned, reached out, and picked up his cup of hot chocolate.

She sipped her own cocoa, gazing at him through lowered lashes as she faced the fact that this man could provoke her in a way no one else had... not even Blake!

Tath lay on his side, one elbow propped on the sofa, to look at her. He smiled and asked, "What's going on behind those big green eyes?"

"I wouldn't tell you for all the money in the world," she replied hastily, and looked away.

"Ah, then maybe I'm making headway."

They drank their chocolate in silence for a moment. Hilary watched the burning logs as one fell, sending a shower of orange sparks up the blackened chimney. Tath asked her, "What do you do for fun?"

She pulled off her boots and set them to one side. Wriggling her toes, she answered, "There really hasn't been time for too many leisure activities. I sew and I like to read."

"Why hasn't there been time?"

She shrugged. "I've worked either part time or full time since I was fourteen years old."

In an easy movement, Tath rose and crossed to take the cup from her hands. "Come dance with me."

He went to a bookcase and turned the dial on the stereo tuner until he found a station playing a classic French ballad.

"And now for the dance floor," he said, kicking a rug and sending it sliding across the polished floor. While he held Hilary's hand, he pushed a glass coffee table out of their way, then pulled her into his arms.

She felt his chin against her temple, his breath on her hair; she thought of Tath's ability to shake her to her toes. Blake had been as blond as Greg Justin, and slightly shorter than Tath, she realized as they swayed slowly in each other's arms. Blake wouldn't have held her wrist in the restaurant. He would have hated Snuffy.

The fleeting memories she conjured up of Blake Crowley faded beneath a gentle, deliberate onslaught of caresses from Tath.

Provoking torment, his fingers traced the curve of her spine until she reached around and caught his hand. His fingers enveloped hers and held them lightly. His lips were soft and warm as they brushed her ear.

His breath teased her as fully as his lips. "You sound positive when you say you don't want my kiss," he whispered, "but you like what I'm doing now. I think that layer of ice is only skin-deep."

"Tath," she murmured, "I don't believe in playing with matches. I don't drive over a hundred and I wouldn't pet a tiger. I might as well be doing all three now."

Every touch of his hands, his breath, his mouth, befuddled her thoughts. Tension built while he deftly stroked the sensitive skin in the hollows of her throat and behind her neck.

Each enticing caress blazed a danger signal, and at the same time demolished her defenses. Her head felt heavy as she leaned back and looked up at him.

"Tath, I feel like Mount Everest—like I'm presenting a big challenge your ego won't let you ignore."

He gazed down at her with hooded eyes. "You know you're a challenge."

"I don't want to be."

"Hilary, don't pull away. I'm not trying to make a conquest."

"Then what *are* you doing?"

His gray eyes darkened and his voice was hoarse with passion. "You're pure temptation." His fingers wound in her soft curls. "You say no, but those green eyes dare me to take possession of your lips again," he whispered.

All her nerves quivered with anticipation. She couldn't resist lifting her face and closing her eyes. She was as hungry for his lips as he was for hers, and when his mouth closed over hers, she felt her insides turn to molten lava.

His arms enclosed her, crushing her to him while her pliant body molded to his lean frame.

In a dizzying rush, she thought, *I should stop,* then, *I must stop him,* and finally a voice in the back of her mind whispered, *I can't...I can't!* She slipped her arms around his neck and arched against him. All her reservations crashed into oblivion.

Through lowered eyelids, she looked at him and saw surprise light his face for an instant before his kiss deepened.

The tempest of pent-up yearnings he had awakened unfurled and she returned his kiss with equal abandon. Pressing against him, she felt a body that was strong and vital. She was filled with a deep yearning to know every inch of that lean frame, every cell of that warm skin, every taut muscle.

"I've wanted to do this since that first kiss in the restaurant," he whispered as with lightning speed his fingers unbuttoned her blouse and expertly unfastened her bra. Before she could anticipate his action, he had cupped her creamy breasts in his hands and his mouth gently teased first one nipple, then the other. The surge of desire that rocked her being was so powerful that it terrified her. Instantly she came to her senses and forced herself to break away from him. With trembling fingers, she refastened her bra and buttoned her blouse. "No, Tath," she beseeched him. "No!" Her eyes pleaded with him to leave her alone.

His face was a study of frustrated desire. His breathing was ragged and his fists were clenched. Whatever he had done to her, it was evident she had aroused the same stormy passions in him.

"Come here," he murmured, and reached for her.

She couldn't get out any words. She shook her head and took a step away. Finally she whispered, "Tath, stop it."

"You can't back away now. You loved what I was doing to you. Your body's message came through loud and clear."

"Don't bully me, Tath. In the morning we'll start working together—I don't want that complicated by emotions or sex."

"It doesn't have to be. If you're professional, it's not difficult to keep your private life separate."

She felt a flash of anger at his attitude. "I see, I haven't learned to compartmentalize my life as you have. Tath, I haven't known you a full twenty-four hours yet. Don't rush me."

He gazed at her a moment. "Okay, but you're asking a lot." He smiled, but there was a grim determination on his face that made her uneasy. A log tumbled and broke in the fireplace and Tath turned to glance at it. He strolled to the hearth, picked up a poker, and moved the screen to jab the logs, sending a spray of sparks up the chimney.

With deliberate movements, taking his time, he replaced the poker and turned to face her. He looked far more composed than he had a few seconds earlier. In a level voice he asked, "Care for another cup of hot chocolate or something else?"

"I'll take a cold drink. Ice water will be fine."

He smiled and held out his hand. "Come on, we'll sit in the kitchen."

She picked up the empty cups. He put his arm around her shoulder. She felt shaken, disturbed, and shocked at her reactions. Relief filled her because he seemed to know she needed time to sort out her feelings about him.

When they entered the kitchen, they heard whining and scratching at the utility room door. "Snuffy needs to get outside," Hilary said.

Tath crossed the room to get the dog and put him in the backyard. As soon as he closed the door, a howl sounded.

Hilary laughed. "He's not the easiest dog to have around. I'd better get his leash and walk him or he'll stay right by that door and howl to get in out of the rain."

"Hell's bells," Tath muttered. "Sit down. I'll do it."

"He's mine. You don't need to get wet..."

Tath crossed the kitchen to the closet to withdraw a raincoat. "I don't know why not. That dog has caused me to get wet more than once already tonight. Not to mention my demolished sweater." He pulled on his raincoat and reached for a leash, which he showed to Hilary. "See, I've got my own leash, and I'm tempted to wrap it around his scrawny neck!"

A mournful howl rose on the other side of the door and they heard a frantic scratching. Hilary was embarrassed, but she also had to fight an urge to laugh.

The phone rang and both of them glanced at it. Tath waved his hand toward it. "Hilary, please get that while I do something about this mutt. Ask who it is and I'll call them back." He placed his hand on the doorknob and glanced over his shoulder at her. "If it's about the mill, come and get me."

As he left, she hurried to the phone. When she answered, a woman's voice asked for Tath. Hilary said he wasn't in and took the message, realizing they both sounded as if it were the middle of the day instead of the early hours of the morning. When she replaced the receiver, she moved to the sink to rinse the cocoa cups.

The door opened and Tath entered, carrying Snuffy, who looked as happy as possible. Tath dried Snuffy's feet before setting him down. Instead of rushing to Hilary as she expected, the terrier sat down and gazed up at Tath.

"I think he's transferring his loyalty," she observed.

Tath looked down at Snuffy. "He's trying to make up for all his crimes." He reached down and scratched the dog's ears.

As if satisfied by the gesture, Snuffy turned and trotted to Hilary. She led him to the utility room, where she saw that Tath had placed a bowl of food, a dish of water, and a pile of towels for a bed. "Try and be good, Snuffy," she whispered.

Snuffy's dark brown eyes gazed at her as he sat down and turned his head to one side. She reached out to scratch his head before rising and turning off the light. When she closed the door, she held her breath, hoping that he wouldn't start howling for her again. To her relief, all was silent.

She looked at Tath. "Natalie called and left a message. I wrote it down and left it beside the phone." She started toward the hall. "I'd like to go to sleep now. Thank you for dinner and the, ah, interesting evening."

He crossed the room and put his arms around her. "It could be a lot more interesting."

She gazed up at him while she tried to ignore the ache of longing she felt inside. "No."

He reached up and lightly touched her hair, moving strands of it away from her face, tucking them behind her ear. "We could be so good to each other, Hilary. Let me love you tonight."

Love! What did he know about love, Hilary thought bitterly. He was only interested in taking her to bed, using her. She pushed determinedly against his chest, but his arms remained around her. She looked up to catch him studying her mouth. She said quickly, "Tath, there's Natalie, Meredith, the woman in the red car, and God knows how many others—you don't need me and I don't want to be part of a harem."

"You're different, Hilary."

"Only because I'm not interested."

His gray eyes glittered and he drawled, "Aren't you?"

She pushed again, hard, and stepped out of his arms. "Good night, Tath." Her heart pounded as she turned to leave for her room. By the time she'd closed her door and turned on the lights, her pulse was normal, but she paced the floor restlessly, thinking about the evening, about Tath and her reaction to him.

She undressed for bed, pulling on a blue satin nightgown before she slipped between the smooth yellow sheets. It was impossible to resist glancing at the door and wondering if Tath was asleep—or tossing and turning as she was. A vision of that lithe, strong body stretched out in bed was agony. She groaned and rubbed her eyes.

After all that had happened tonight, how could she work with him and still keep her sanity? Memories of the evening crowded in. Each feathery touch of his fingertips and lips might as well have been branded on her skin. And the charm of the man was monumental. He had only to look at her with those smoky eyes and she felt utterly vulnerable. She groaned and turned over. It was hours before she dozed, to have disturbing dreams of long-lashed gray eyes and a rich baritone voice.

- 7 -

SHE AWOKE TO a dark, cloudy dawn. Listening to the silence, she realized she should let Snuffy outside, so she pulled on a blue organdy robe and descended the stairs. When she entered the kitchen, she halted in surprise. Dressed in jeans, with his chest bare, Tath leaned against the counter and held a cup of coffee.

The room was warm, filled with the smell of fresh coffee. From a radio on the kitchen counter came the morning news. "I didn't know you were up," Hilary said in surprise. "I came downstairs to let Snuffy out."

"He's already outside. I fed him, too."

She faced Tath again, watching his eyes appraise her languorously until she felt as if her robe and gown had just been stripped away. She touched her collar.

"Care for coffee?" Tath asked.

She nodded and he turned to pour it for her.

"Did you sleep well?" he asked huskily.

Why did his merest glance turn her legs to jelly? She glanced at his mouth and remembered exactly how it felt on hers. She licked her lips. With a quick motion, he took the coffee cup from her hands and set it down.

"I didn't sleep worth a damn," he muttered as he pulled her to him. He leaned down to kiss her while her hands slid across his bare shoulders into the thick curls on the back of his head.

Hilary could hear only the pounding of her heart. She never heard footsteps or the door or anyone until a voice broke over them.

"Tath!"

He loosened his hold and turned. Hilary stepped away

77

and looked at the two people staring at her.

Beside Tath's brother, Greg, stood a strikingly attractive woman whose exquisitely coiffed brown hair was softened by touches of gray. She wore a quietly expensive navy dress, and her high cheekbones and sculpted features added to her patrician air. Beneath the woman's raised eyebrows, the same gray eyes as Tath's were unmistakable. Next to her stood Greg, carrying three suitcases. As he lowered them to the floor, he said, chuckling, "No wonder you gave me the slip last night, little brother."

Even though Tath ignored the comment, Hilary burned with embarrassment at being found in Tath's arms, wearing only a gown and robe.

"Hilary, this is my mother," Tath said. "Mother, this is Hilary O'Brien."

"Good morning," Mrs. Justin remarked in such a cold voice that Hilary felt a knot inside. With a sinking feeling, she noticed the flush on Mrs. Justin's cheeks and she thought of the similarity between this woman and Blake Crowley's mother. Both were attractive widows who looked, dressed, and talked with the confidence of old money and aristocratic pedigrees. And in Mrs. Justin's cool tones, Hilary heard the same veiled hostility toward herself that Mrs. Crowley had always shown her.

Hilary tried to sound composed as she acknowledged the greeting. "I'm glad to meet you, Mrs. Justin."

Tath spoke easily. His voice sounded normal. "Hilary is with a production company in Dallas. She'll be doing some commercials for Justin Mills. Elliot hired her and asked her to stay here while working on the project."

"Elliot!" Mrs. Justin's eyes narrowed. "How long have you been at my house, Miss O'Brien?"

Hilary didn't miss the emphasis on the words "my house." She raised her chin and replied, "I came yesterday."

"Yesterday!"

"Mother, would you like a cup of coffee?" Tath asked.

"Indeed not. Have you forgotten, Tath, that we're having forty guests for a party tonight?"

Greg whistled. "I forgot!"

Mrs. Justin glanced at him quickly. "You both promised you'd attend."

"I'll be here for it," Greg answered.

She looked at her younger son. "Tath?"

"I'll come, Mother. How was your trip?"

"Fine until this morning." She looked at his brother. "Put those in my room, Greg." She glanced around. "Where is everyone, Tath? Lena and Beatrice should both be here. Why haven't they started cooking for tonight?"

"I told them they wouldn't be needed until nine o'clock."

"Oh, for heaven's sake! It's a good thing I'm home."

Hilary spoke up. "Mrs. Justin, I think perhaps I'd better move to a hotel. I can see that my presence is an inconvenience to you."

"Hilary—" Tath began, but his mother interrupted him.

"Tath, why don't you call the Hotel St. Jean and make a reservation for Miss O'Brien."

"That's all right," Hilary said quickly. "I can make my own reservation. I'll be leaving shortly anyway."

Mrs. Justin's slate-colored eyes rested on her. "It was nice to meet you, Miss O'Brien," she said in an uncompromising tone that Hilary felt conveyed an entirely different message.

Helplessly, Hilary watched the older woman leave the room, feeling she'd made a poor impression. She heard the back door rattle and Elliot Compton entered the kitchen.

His wide blue eyes looked as harmless as the bouquet on the kitchen table, and he greeted her with a wide smile.

"Morning, Hilary, Tath. I had arranged to pick up your mother at the airport, but apparently Greg didn't know that. Here, I stopped at the mailbox to pick up your morning paper." He handed it to Tath, who tossed the newspaper onto the table.

Tath frowned at Greg. "How thoughtful of you to meet Mother and bring her home at such an early hour, especially when she already had a ride."

Greg grinned, but remained quiet as Elliot Compton said, "Tath, I got a call last night from Roger that the mill's flooded."

"Before the night was over, it was probably in two feet of water," Tath said. "As soon as I eat breakfast, I'm going out there. Did he tell you we put that new equipment on the trucks?"

"Yes," Elliot answered. "He said you rescued the files from the office, too."

From the living room, Mrs. Justin's voice rose in an anguished cry. "Tath!"

With an apologetic shrug, Tath rushed from the room. Greg followed, and Elliot Compton said, "If you'll excuse me, Hilary, I'll go with them."

Nodding, Hilary felt as if she had been buffeted by a storm. She started for her room, paused, and listened as she heard a series of sharp barks and another agonized cry from Mrs. Justin. Tath's deep voice yelled, "Snuffy!"

Hilary's heart seemed to rise to her throat. She rushed to the living room, where she paused in the doorway.

All of Snuffy's previous antics and escapades paled to insignificance. Hilary couldn't move. She gazed at the horror in front of her while inside she cringed with shame.

The furniture and rug were covered with feathers. In the center of the room stood Mrs. Justin, red-faced, shrieking and pointing her finger at the dog while Tath and Greg circled a rose-colored sofa. The object of their pursuit remained between the two men, poised, ready to dodge, wagging his tail while he held what had been a lovely, silk-embroidered pillow between his teeth.

"Oh, Snuffy, no!" Hilary whispered, and promised herself that she'd never take in another stray animal, no matter how starved it looked.

Elliot Compton stood nearby, chuckling and rocking on his heels.

"Snuffy, come here!" Tath said. His brow furrowed as he glared at the dog.

"That monster!" Mrs. Justin exclaimed, wiping her nose. "My pillows!"

Hilary rushed forward. "Snuffy! Come here to me!"

Tath lunged for the terrier. Snuffy dodged and scooted beneath the high Provincial sofa to slip through to the other side. Greg reached for him, and Snuffy ran around the sofa to confront Tath again.

Hilary joined in the chase. As she neared Tath, she asked, "How did he get in here? I thought you had him shut in the utility room."

"I let him into the kitchen after he'd been outside; I planned to put him in the utility room, but I wanted to make coffee first." He straightened and looked into her eyes. "Then you came in and I forgot everything."

For an instant she forgot Snuffy, because she knew Tath was referring to their kiss. When the terrier dodged for a chair, she returned her attention to him at the same time Tath did.

Tath made a dive and scooped up the wriggling dog. Hilary stepped forward to take him, but Tath tightened his hold. "I have him."

She turned and felt everything inside freeze as she faced the fury in Mrs. Justin's blazing eyes.

"Mrs. Justin, I'm so sorry..."

Tath's arm fell across her shoulders. In a firm voice, he interrupted. "Mother, I'll take care of all this. Hilary didn't have anything to do with the dog getting in here. I let him in."

"This beautiful room is destroyed!" Mrs. Justin exclaimed.

"We can replace the pillows and get the room clean," Tath continued calmly, "so don't worry about it."

Mrs. Justin's cheeks were red, and her gray eyes had darkened. "We have forty guests coming tonight and they'll all be in this room. My beautiful pillows..."

Snuffy barked at her, a series of yips that brought a deeper frown to Mrs. Justin's face.

"Get that animal out of this room, Tath."

"Sure, but you come too. I'll see to all this mess."

Hilary watched Elliot walk out of the room with Greg. Mrs. Justin whirled and left behind them. As Tath started to follow her, Hilary touched his arm.

"I have to clean this up myself. I feel responsible; I can't just leave it to someone else."

"Yes, you can. It's just feathers, and a vacuum will take them up in minutes."

She felt mortified by Snuffy's behavior, and knew the consequences wouldn't be as light as Tath thought. She turned a reproving gaze on the terrier and said, "Snuffy, you're in big trouble."

As if he understood her words, the dog whined and Tath laughed. "Poor Snuffy! How was he to know those pillows weren't meant for him?" He scratched the dog's ears while Snuffy wagged his tail.

"Tath, I've really got to tidy up the mess," Hilary reminded him.

He smiled at her. "All right, if cleaning it up yourself will make you feel better, I'll get the vacuum and take Snuffy outside."

As soon as he was gone, Hilary began picking up ripped swatches of blue silk embroidered with what she guessed were tiny yellow, pink, and white flowers. She found part of a rose velvet pillow and reached for it as Greg entered the room.

"You don't need to do that."

She straightened and looked at him as he stood with one hand in his pocket, relaxed and amused. "So I've heard," she said, and turned to pick up some more pieces of fabric.

"Hilary, are you in love with Tath?" Greg asked abruptly.

"No! I just met him yesterday," she answered without thinking.

Greg looked down at her robe and she flushed, remembering that he'd caught her in Tath's arms only a few minutes ago.

She didn't care to explain anything to Greg Justin, but he smiled at her and strolled closer.

He said, "There's a sternwheeler on the Mississippi you might enjoy. Have dinner with me tonight."

Carrying an upright vacuum cleaner and attachments, Tath spoke from the doorway. "Hilary's promised to come to Mother's party with me—and you promised Mother you'd be there, too."

In consternation, Hilary gazed at Tath. She didn't want

to go out with Greg Justin, yet she didn't like Tath's announcement when he hadn't consulted her.

Greg watched her a moment until she said, "I'm sorry, Greg."

He shrugged. "Well, I'll leave you two to your cleaning fun. See you tonight."

Tath straightened and said, "I'm going to the mill in just a few minutes. Are you going now?"

"I'll stop for breakfast first."

She saw Tath's jaw harden and knew Greg's answer had annoyed him, but he began unwinding the cord to the vacuum.

When he switched on the appliance, Hilary crossed to him and turned it off. He raised his eyebrows and she explained, "Thanks for saving me from a difficult moment, but I don't have a date with you tonight. I don't expect to hold you to that."

He grinned. "Oh, no. You can't back out now. When you didn't deny it, you became my accomplice after the fact."

She felt conflicting emotions. She wanted to spend the evening with him, yet at the same time she was aggravated by his assumption that she would. Furthermore, she didn't want to attend Mrs. Justin's party, with or without a date.

"You're very dictatorial, you know?" she told him.

His grin widened. "I didn't want you to accept Greg's offer."

Unable to resist, she laughed. "You're hopeless!"

"I take it that means you'll go with me."

She had to say, "Your mother isn't going to want me."

"She needs to get to know you."

"When I move out this morning, I'll never see her again."

"You might," he answered easily.

She wondered what he meant, but saw that he wasn't going to elaborate, so she reached for the vacuum.

"You get the feathers off those tables and I'll do this," he said, switching on the vacuum and drowning out any answer she might make.

Finally the room was once again in order. Hilary straightened and pushed her hair away from her face. "Now are you going to tell me where I go to get those pillows," she asked, "or do I have to get the information from your mother?"

He looked down at her. "It won't do any good to tell you that no one will miss the pillows, they don't need to be replaced, or that I'll take care of it?"

"No. If you don't tell me, I'll have to ask your mother, which I'd rather not do. You can spare both of us that interview."

He shrugged. "All right, but it isn't necessary."

He stepped into the hall and returned with a slip of paper and a pen. Hilary watched him scribble a name as he explained, "He's the decorator who did those pillows for Mother." He wrote down the address and then handed her the scrap of paper.

"Tath, your mother isn't going to want me at her party after what Snuffy did."

He looked amused. "Let me worry about that." He reached out and touched her collar, smoothing it while he talked. "I'm going to the mill, and I'll probably be busy for about three hours. Why don't I pick you up at the Hotel St. Jean about eleven o'clock and we'll start on the commercials?"

"I'll meet you at the mill," she said.

"Suit yourself." He turned to gather up the vacuum and attachments. "Oh, by the way, they don't allow pets at the St. Jean—or at any of the other good hotels, for that matter. But I know a place to board Snuffy, if you can bear to be separated from him."

She sighed. "After all the trouble he's caused, a breather might be good for both Snuffy and me. If you'll just give me the address of the kennel—"

"Oh, I'll take him over and get him settled," Tath offered quickly. "You have your packing and moving to do. I'll give you the address of the place later, so you can visit him."

"Thank you," Hilary acquiesced. "I'm sorry to put you to so much trouble, Tath."

"No trouble," he said easily. "And don't let Mother's attitude upset you. She wasn't too keen when Dad brought home the collie without consulting her, and she's had a grudge against all dogs ever since."

And now she has a grudge against me, Hilary thought, but she only gave Tath a wan smile. Taking her arm, he led her from the living room and walked her down the hall to the staircase. "See you at eleven," he said cheerily as she started up the stairs.

As quickly as she could, Hilary bathed, dressed, and packed. Finally, after the car was loaded with her things and she'd made a reservation at the St. Jean, she looked for Mrs. Justin and found her arranging a vase of flowers in the solarium.

Tath's mother had changed to pale green slacks and a white blouse. She frowned as Hilary entered the room.

"Mrs. Justin, I'm ready to leave now, and I wanted to tell you again how sorry I am about my dog. Tath gave me Mr. Weldon's name and I'll replace the pillows."

Poised over a vase of carnations, Mrs. Justin straightened. "Thank you. He'll know what I want."

There seemed to be little more to say except, "I'm glad to have met you."

Mrs Justin smiled frostily. "Good-bye, Miss O'Brien."

Hilary felt dismissed. She turned away, wishing she had firmly refused Tath's invitation for the evening. But she was now committed to attend the party, and could only hope that no further ordeal with the Justins lay ahead.

- *8* -

AFTER CHECKING INTO the Hotel St. Jean and unpacking her things, Hilary drove to Chez Jacques and went to Jack Nalley's office to pay half the bill for the previous evening's damages to the restaurant. After a brief argument, she gave up when the restaurateur refused to accept a check from her, explaining that Mr. Justin had already taken care of the matter. Next she drove to a store that carried the brand of sweaters Snuffy had chewed to pieces. After buying an identical blue sweater for Tath, she returned to her car to drive to the decorator's. When she wrote a check for the cost of the pillows that he promised to make and deliver to the Justins', Hilary decided Snuffy was an expensive pet.

Finally she headed for the mill, driving through residential districts that gradually changed to busier industrial areas. The sun shone brightly on streets filled with puddles of water; weeds and sticks and strands of grass were caught high on posts and fences where the floodwaters had deposited them the night before. The area smelled like sour laundry, and the foundations of the buildings were darkened from mud.

She passed a warehouse where muddy water was being pumped out through large hoses, spurting into the street in sluggish streams while men worked carrying equipment outside into the sun.

When she turned into the parking lot, it was filled with cars, equipment, and activity. She drove past a row of cars until she found an empty slot. Picking up the box containing the sweater, she climbed out of her car and was heading toward the back door when Tath came out with a man in a gray business suit. Hilary watched as the two stopped to talk.

At the sight of Tath, who was dressed in a navy suit and pale blue shirt, she felt her stomach do a flip-flop. His brown hair curled above his forehead and he pushed open his coat while he talked, placing his hand in his pocket. He looked relaxed and full of confidence.

Mentally, she warned herself to take care. She shouldn't have such a reaction to a man she'd known less than twenty-four hours, much less a man who was an infamous playboy. As she drew closer, he glanced around and saw her. She heard him tell the other man good-bye, and then he turned to stroll in her direction.

While the distance between them narrowed, she was aware of his scrutiny. When she reached him, he took both of her hands and remarked, "My, you look lovely."

She smiled. "Thank you, but I suspect you say that the way others say hello."

"Not quite." He leaned forward to brush her cheek with his lips. "You smell lovely, too."

"Thank you again. How's the mill?"

He frowned. "Not good. The adjustor just left. It's heavily damaged and I don't know what we'll be able to do about the commercials, because things aren't back to normal. I'd show you around now, but you're far too clean to go through it." He glanced down at her green linen pumps. "Those pretty green shoes would turn brown."

"How about showing me one of the Justin farms?" she suggested. "We talked about that before, maybe starting with a shot of cotton in the field."

He rubbed the back of his neck a moment before nodding, "All right, but that may be muddy, too. Why don't we stop by the St. Jean so you can change into jeans?"

"Fine." She extended the box. "Here, this is yours."

He took the box, glanced at the name stamped in the corner, and looked at her while he opened it. He pulled out the new blue sweater.

"I appreciate your thoughtfulness, but you really didn't

have to replace the sweater, Hilary," he told her.

"Oh, yes, I did," she said firmly.

He looked at the soft material. "You know, the old one wasn't a particular favorite of mine, but this one will be— because it's from you." His gray eyes caressed her warmly.

She dropped her gaze, suddenly self-conscious. "At least you won't have to worry about Snuffy destroying it. By the way, where is he?"

"Safe and sound," Tath assured her. "I'll give you details later. Look," he went on hurriedly, "I've got a pair of jeans in the office. If you'll wait in my car, I'll change here, drive you to the hotel, and we can be on our way. When we're through, I'll bring you back here to get your car. How's that?"

She was anxious to know of her dog's whereabouts, but didn't want to press the subject when Tath was obviously in a rush to get to the farm, so she merely nodded. He handed her the box with the sweater. "Put this in the car. And, Hilary, thank you for the gift."

"You're welcome." She took the box and walked to his car to wait. In a few minutes she saw him coming out the door. He was dressed in tight jeans and a blue knit shirt that fit smoothly across his broad shoulders.

In a second he slid behind the wheel and started the car to take her to the hotel, where she changed to jeans and a plaid blouse. She joined Tath again and they drove out of town. The farm was a short distance from the city. The main house sat high on a bluff overlooking the Mississippi River.

Hilary looked at row upon row of sturdy cotton plants while Tath leaned against a rail fence. "When the Spanish came to America," he said, "they found Pima Indians growing cotton. Columbus took some cotton yarn back to Queen Isabella as a New World artifact." He squinted as he gazed across the field. "Cotton is the most widely used fiber in the world, and I think its use will continue to increase. We can control shrinkage and we've made it wash-and-wear."

He was silent a moment as he looked at the plants, then he said, "It all begins here."

"Then we'll begin here, too." Hilary remarked, and made notes in a tablet. "We'll start with a shot of these fields, emphasize that it's a natural fiber. You said you wanted to promote cotton as a product of Louisiana. Can we drive around so I can look for some likely settings for pictures?"

"Sure." He straightened and dropped his arm across her shoulders as they walked back to the car. Tath drove along a narrow, rough dirt road past acres of cotton. He stopped at the farmhouse and introduced Hilary to the Smiths, the people who managed the farm. After a cup of coffee with the Smiths, they returned to Tath's Porsche for another drive, on which Hilary saw hybridization labs, long rows of greenhouses for growing experimental plants.

While he drove, Tath said, "After the cotton is picked it goes to a gin to remove the fibers from the seeds. Inside the gin, a comb blocks the seeds and lets the fibers pass through. These fibers, or lint, are pressed into one-hundred-pound bales and sent to our mill. By tomorrow I should be able to take you on a tour of the mill. Even if the machines aren't operating, you can get an idea what it's like. Tomorrow night we'll go sight-seeing again. Okay with you?"

"Fine." She gazed past the row of labs and saw a barn filled with equipment. Beyond, fields of cotton disappeared over the horizon.

To the west of a cotton field was a row of oaks festooned with Spanish moss. When she saw it, Hilary made another notation in her tablet. Tath glanced down and asked, "What are you writing?"

"I'm making notes about likely places to film. When this week is over, I'll take all this back to the office and start a storyboard." She pointed toward the field. "I made notes about this setting. Live oaks behind the cotton might make a good scene because it would convey a sense of Louisiana."

He glanced at the thin gold watch on his wrist. "How about scheduling lunch now? I'm famished, and that cup of coffee was no substitute for a meal."

She nodded. "Sounds good."

They left the farm and drove along the highway until they came to a restaurant. While Tath ate broiled flounder,

Hilary had crayfish bisque and hot coffee. She tried one more time to get out of the party at his mother's house.

"Tath, let's cancel the date tonight. Your mother isn't going to be happy to see me."

"You said you'd go and I won't let you back out." He studied her a minute. "Tell me about your engagement to Blake Crowley. Was it long ago or recently?"

She shrugged. "It's been more than a year."

"How long were you engaged?"

She didn't particularly mind the questions; his tone of voice expressed a need to understand her better, rather than mere curiosity. "Four months."

"Where did you meet him?"

"He's a Boston lawyer, and I went to work as a secretary for a friend of his. The friend introduced us and we started dating." She was certain he wanted to know why her engagement had ended, but she didn't care to tell him that Blake's family hadn't approved of her. She knew that was why she was so sensitive to Mrs. Justin's coldness, and she wondered if she would ever forget Mrs. Crowley's snubs and unkind remarks. She gazed down at the cup of coffee and stirred cream into it while she remembered Blake and the last argument, the night of a dance at his country club. He'd spent most of the evening away from Hilary, and finally, when they were in the car, she'd asked him where he'd been, why he'd left her alone.

Blake had parked in front of her apartment and turned to her, his dark eyes resting on her while he said, "I was talking with the Daniels about their trip to the Bahamas. You don't know them or their friends, and I knew you wouldn't be interested. You don't always fit in, Hilary."

She glanced up at Tath as she remembered Blake's words. At the time, the pain had been terrible. His declaration that she didn't fit in had started an argument until finally he told her coldly and flatly that he wanted to break the engagement. A month later he was engaged to the socially acceptable Emily Devon.

After a moment, Tath asked, "How old is Blake Crowley?" Instantly she recalled her statement about preferring older

men. Since Blake was four years younger than Tath, he
hardly qualified, but she didn't want her lie to be exposed.
"He's old enough," she replied vaguely.

Tath gazed at her. "That's suspiciously evasive, Hilary.
How old?"

She knew that if she admitted Blake's age, Tath would
quiz her about her reason for saying she preferred older
men. Now she wished she'd never made up any such statement, but she was caught in a web of her own weaving.
"He's just slightly bald," she said.

Inwardly she groaned at the sight of Tath's eyes widening
in surprise. How she wished she'd never made that remark
about older men! She thought of Blake's full head of thick,
curly blond hair. She wanted to change the subject and tried
to think of a topic, but before she could, Tath spoke.

"The fact that he's bald doesn't mean anything. How old
is he?"

She was in too deep to get out now. It seemed hopeless,
and she muttered, "Thirty-eight."

She'd just added ten years to Blake's life and removed
his hair. It was also one of the few times in her life she had
ever lied to someone, and she swore to herself it would be
the last.

At least Tath's questions ceased. He seemed lost in
thought, probably meditating on a fascinating thirty-eight-
year-old, baldheaded man who didn't exist.

Tath studied her and rubbed his chin while he spoke so
softly she could barely hear his words. "I'm too young, I
obviously don't appeal to you the way some men do, I
apparently don't have a personality that is compatible with
yours. I don't mean it in a conceited way, Hilary, but I
don't usually bomb out this badly."

Stricken with remorse, she answered honestly, "You hav-
en't bombed out, Tath."

"My God, Hilary! You sound as if you pity me!"

She thought of his teasing and occasional dictatorial manner and began to enjoy herself. She grinned across the table
at him and said consolingly, "Tath, you're really very attractive."

He looked at her intently for such a long time that she wondered if he'd misunderstood what she had said. Why didn't he move or say something, she wondered. Finally he remarked in quiet tones, "You think so, Hilary?"

"Of course. You have a regular harem and they seem to adore you, so what does one more woman's opinion matter? I think you're nice." She enjoyed every word, and his silent reception.

He raised an eyebrow and muttered, "Nice!" After a moment he added, "Perhaps on further acquaintance, your opinion of me will improve. Are you ready to go now?"

She felt satisfied. Tath Justin had caused her more trouble than anyone else except Blake. Blake had hurt her and brought her anguish, but he hadn't made sparks fly and aggravated her the way Tath had, and she found her mild revenge exhilarating.

When they left the restaurant and walked to the car, Tath remained silent. All the time that he held the car door for her and walked around to climb in and sit behind the wheel, he didn't speak. He maintained his silence even as they drove away.

She chatted about the scenery, blithely remarking about oaks and Spanish moss, the French Quarter, and the farm they'd visited earlier. He seemed preoccupied, and she guessed he was still brooding over their conversation in the restaurant. As he whipped into the empty parking lot at the mill, she turned to look at him. "I didn't realize it was so late."

"The clean-up crew's finished and gone," he said. Beneath the late-afternoon sun, he slid to a stop next to her car.

"There's no need to drive to the hotel to pick me up and drive back to your house," she said. "I'll meet you there."

He turned off the engine and turned to look at her. "I'll come get you, because I've moved out, too. Today my houseboat was delivered."

While he talked, his intense scrutiny made her draw a sharp breath and she wondered if she'd gone too far with her patronizing remarks to him. She had a suspicion that her studied indifference might merely make her seem even more of a challenge to his ego, and suddenly she wanted to get out of his car and into her own. She started to open the door, but he spoke and she paused.

Stretching his legs, he rummaged in the pocket of his jeans. "I'll give you my boat phone number. I don't even know it, because the phones were installed only this morning." He pulled out a piece of paper. "Do you have something to write on?"

She opened her purse and pulled out one of her business cards to write on the back of it, making a note of the numbers that Tath read aloud to her. She glanced at it and said, "I'll give you my room number. Let me get another card." She flipped through the billfold, turning past pictures, credit cards, and money. Finally she withdrew one of the small white cards with her office phone number printed in black.

Too late, she realized what she'd done. The same moment that the realization dawned on her, Tath reached over and turned the plastic compartments of the billfold, thumbing past credit cards to a snapshot.

Her heart began to drum and she tried to retrieve the billfold. He moved a few inches, shifting away from her reach while he glanced at her before looking down again at the picture in his hands.

Helplessly she watched him study the picture of her smiling into the camera with Blake. He was dressed in a knit shirt, his blond hair ruffled by the wind, and his face looking even more boyish than his twenty-seven years at the time the picture was taken.

The devilish glint in Tath's eyes transformed her embarrassment to nervousness. He drawled, "Is this your bald-headed, thirty-eight-year-old ex-fiancé, Blake Crowley?"

She licked dry lips. "Tath, I was teasing..."

He closed the billfold, studying her intently. "How old is Blake?"

She drew a shaky breath. "Tath..." At the piercing look from his steel-gray eyes, she admitted the truth. "He's twenty-eight."

"That's a healthy head of hair," Tath remarked dryly.

From the first moment she'd encountered Tath, with her head under his bed while she tried to get Snuffy, everything between them had ended in disaster. And she knew she was headed for another calamity now.

She couldn't think of a thing to say while she watched him close the billfold, tuck it into her purse, and look up at her.

In a mocking voice he said, "So you like men who are over thirty-five, your ex-fiancé is thirty-eight and balding . . ."

With each damning word coming back at her, she felt warmth suffuse her face. The wicked glitter in Tath's eye sent her pulse racing as he edged closer.

"You don't like my kisses, you think I'm merely 'nice'— why did you tell me all that, Hilary?" His hand slipped across her shoulder, behind her neck, and tugged gently. His knees pressed against hers as he inched nearer.

His voice dropped. "Are you a compulsive liar? Do you always tell such whoppers?"

Her heartbeat drummed in her ears and she put her hands against his chest. "No, Tath . . ."

"Why did you fabricate such monumental lies?" His other hand slipped around her waist and he drew her to him. While those stony gray eyes pierced through her, he demanded in a deep voice, "Why did you do it Hilary?"

"I'm sorry. I shouldn't have."

Amusement raised the corner's of his mouth into a sardonic smile. "If I'm so damned 'nice' and safe and unappealing and young, why go to all that trouble? Why tell me such nonsense about your ex-fiancé?" He leaned closer until he was only inches away. "Why?"

"To keep you from doing what you're doing now," she stated honestly. She felt consumed by his predatory gaze. Her voice dropped to a whisper. "Because you're a threat to my peace of mind. You're aggravating."

His lips brushed hers briefly. She closed her eyes and whispered, "You're arrogant . . ."

His warm lips were persistent, silencing her words while he pulled her to him. When he raised his head a little, she added, "You're a compulsive womanizer and it doesn't mean anything to you when you kiss me."

"You think this doesn't mean anything?" he whispered.

His arms tightened and he kissed her passionately, sending an electrifying tingle through her. He shifted slightly and she opened her eyes to find his face only inches away. She didn't know when she'd wrapped her arms around his neck.

"You almost blasted my ego to smithereens, you know," he murmured.

"That's impossible."

He studied her for a moment, then reached across her to open the car door.

She was startled by his abruptness. Trying to gather her wits, she watched him while she felt both relief and regret. "Are you angry?"

Looking amused, he trailed his finger along her cheek to the corner of her mouth. "I've always heard that revenge is sweet. You can wonder about it until tonight."

The familiar sense of provocation that he could so easily stir rose again at his evasive answer. For an instant she felt like telling him to forget their date, but before she did, he laughed softly.

"I can see the fire flashing in those sea-green eyes. There's never a dull moment with you, Hilary. I'll pick you up at seven-thirty." He pushed open the door and she climbed out.

He closed the door, started his car, and drove away. Feeling a mixture of emotions—anger, perturbation, longing, and embarrassment—she watched him. When a breeze whipped her hair away from her face, she turned around and walked to her car.

Glancing over her shoulder, she saw Tath waiting at the edge of the lot. She realized he wasn't going to leave her alone, but he hadn't wanted to pursue their conversation.

A tingle of excitement went through her because she

knew he'd come back to it. He'd want to know exactly what she felt for him. As she backed her car, turned, and headed out, she wondered what she did feel. Without reaching any conclusion, she drove past him and waved, smiling at him as if she hadn't a care in the world. He turned his car to follow her until she reached the intersection where she turned north.

Mulling over her reactions to Tath, she was certain of one thing: she didn't want to fall in love with him. He had too many women, was too much of a Don Juan. Even stronger was the realization that his background was the same as Blake's. There were too many similarities between Mrs. Justin and Mrs. Crowley, and Hilary didn't want to repeat the humiliation of her experience with Blake. She didn't want to fall in love with Tath Justin, but in her heart she admitted that he seemed to hold a near fatal attraction for her. She must resist it, especially now that he was her employer.

It was only when the black Porsche had dropped from sight on the busy thoroughfare that she realized she had never asked Tath what he had done with Snuffy.

- 9 -

WHEN SHE REACHED her room, Hilary studied the notes she'd taken during their tour of the Justin farm and the sketches she'd made. Twice she lowered the pad to gaze into space. Accustomed to having Snuffy curled up in the chair beside her or in her lap while she worked at home, she missed him more than ever, and each time she thought of him, she had to make an effort to get her attention back on her work. As soon as Tath picked her up, she would ask about the terrier.

After an hour, she stopped reviewing her notes and started to get dressed for her dinner date with Tath. She selected a soft black sleeveless crepe dress with a round neck. Wearing high-heeled black pumps, a thin gold chain around her neck, and a gold bracelet to match, she brushed her hair, put on a dab of perfume, and descended to the lobby.

She spotted Tath as soon as she stepped out of the elevator. His smoldering gaze as she approached told her that he approved of her appearance. And it was mutual. He wore a dark blue blazer, dark slacks, and a white shirt. How handsome he looked!

Strolling to her, he put his hands on her shoulders and gazed at her for a moment before he leaned forward slightly. "You smell nice, too," he said.

She laughed. "Thank you. Am I supposed to guess what that 'too' means?"

He smiled. "You know exactly. It means you look gorgeous, you smell delectable, and to hell with Mother's dinner party. I want to take you off alone where I don't have to look at or talk to anyone else."

Even though his words and his devouring appraisal filled her with warmth and excitement, she answered calmly, "No, you can't do that. You promised her you'd be there."

He said mockingly. "All afternoon you told me you didn't want to go. Now, when I give you an opportunity to get out of it, you tell me we have to attend."

She smiled and said, "I'm not certain I'm ready to go off alone with you."

One eyebrow curved in question. "Why not?"

"I remember your saying something about sweet revenge."

His voice dropped and became husky as he said, "I'll still get that, whether we go to Mother's or not."

The intimate warmth in his voice made her insides feel as if they were curling into a tight ball.

"How long are we going to stand here in the hotel lobby discussing it?" she asked.

"I'm too dazzled to move."

She laughed and shifted slightly. "That's ridiculous— and nice!"

He smiled and leaned forward to kiss the tip of her nose. "Come on, Hilary. We may as well get this over with."

Taking her arm, he led her outside to the Porsche. Once they were seated in the car, she turned to ask, "How's the mill?"

"I talked to Greg and it's still in bad shape, but part of the equipment is back to normal. Some of the machines are high enough off the floor that water didn't damage them, but we'll still have a big loss. I'm trying not to brood about it—instead, I've been diverting myself with plans for that oceanographic expedition I mentioned to you."

She gazed out the car window at the lengthening shadows of buildings. It was a warm spring evening; traffic had thinned. She turned to ask, "What will you do when you reach the Antarctic?"

"There are five scientists on this trip, and each of us has certain areas of study. Mine is animal life, particularly penguins. I'll be studying trends in their population and how they're being affected by increasing global pollution. South of the equator, seasons are reversed, so by going next November, we'll be there during the Antarctic summer."

"Will all of you study penguins?"

He shook his head. "No. We'll have two meteorologists, a biologist who'll work closely with me, and an ionospheric physicist."

"Are they all single?"

He glanced at her. "No. Only two of us are. One wife is going along—she's a meteorologist. That isn't my only reason for opposing Mother's and Elliot's efforts to get me married."

"You told me you don't want to be tied down."

"That's right, not to the mill, or to a wife that Elliot and Mother have selected for me, nor do I want to give up my expeditions, but those reasons aren't the only ones."

"They seem sufficient," she remarked dryly, and wondered why she'd ever brought up the subject. It sounded as if she were burning with curiosity about his feelings on marriage. In an effort to change the subject to something more neutral, she asked, "How will you study penguins?"

He looked amused, as if he guessed the reason for her deep interest in penguins, but he answered, "We'll band them, examine them for parasites, make observations on nesting habits, that sort of thing." He glanced at her. "Now, on the other subject—getting married and why I don't want to—there are myriad reasons. For starters, I don't want a life like my brother's. He's had four wives who've caused terrible court battles, he pays staggering sums in alimony and child support, and he doesn't see his children often. Although most people wouldn't guess it, Greg isn't a happy person. I don't want to mess up my life that way."

"But you're not Greg," she observed quietly. "Perhaps he's merely married in haste and repented at leisure, as they say. Not that it's any of my business, but I'd guess that you enjoy your harem too much to give it up."

"You keep referring to my 'harem,'" he said with annoyance. "I assure you, Hilary, I don't see myself as some kind of modern-day sheik. But it's true that I haven't yet found one woman who meets all my needs and I won't get married just to please my mother or to do the conventional thing or whatever."

"No one could accuse you of being conventional, Tath," she said wryly.

"Look," he said defensively, "I'm only thirty-two. I have enough on my mind between the expansion of Justin Mills and the oceanographic expedition without adding a wife and maybe kids to worry about. I just don't have time or energy to give to a family of my own right now, Hilary."

"Are you trying to convince me or yourself, Tath?" she challenged him. "Your reasons for remaining single all sound excellent to me."

As they approached a busy intersection, she studied him. Occupied with driving, he could give only a limited amount of attention to her, which made it seem the safest time to bring up something that had bothered her since late afternoon. She said, "Tath, I owe you an apology for telling you that Blake is thirty-eight. I apologize for all those things I said, but I said them in self-defense."

She shifted to look at him. "You're more than 'nice.' You're exciting, too much so. I'm not looking for a husband, but I don't want to be added to a collection of women, either. I was just trying to protect myself."

The light changed to green before Tath reached the intersection. While he continued through it, he glanced at her. Beyond him a car ran the red light, heading directly at them. Hilary yelped and Tath's head whipped around.

"Tath! Look out!" Hilary cried, stiffening with fear.

Tath stepped on the gas and the Porsche sped forward while the other car passed within inches behind them.

Hilary leaned back against the seat. For a moment she felt drained and shaken; she had felt certain they'd collide.

"That was close—and all your fault."

She straightened to look at him. "My fault!"

He kept his eyes on the road. "You distracted me."

She tilted her head to one side to watch him while she remembered her remark that she found him exciting. "I find that a little difficult to believe, but it won't happen again."

He glanced at her and grinned. "Oh, I hope it does, but not in the center of a busy intersection. Tell me again when I'm not driving."

She laughed. "That's exactly why I picked that moment to tell you, only I didn't know it might have disastrous consequences!"

"It's a wonder I didn't run into a light pole!"

She smiled. "I think the blame lies more with that man who ran the red light."

They turned into the drive at the Justin house. The mansion looked as if it had a light in every window. Lights blazed on the drive and the wide veranda, and Hilary thought again of the similarity between Blake and Tath. The most dangerous similarity was her involvement again with a wealthy, socially prominent man whose mother was a dominant influence in his life.

Along the drive which was lined with parked cars, Tath slowed and headed behind the house to park in front of the garage. He glanced at her. "You've suddenly become very quiet. What's going on in that mind of yours?"

She looked at him and forced lightness into her voice. "That, Mr. Justin, is a deep, dark secret."

He cut the motor and turned to take her chin in his hand. "I can't figure you out. Every time I think I have you neatly pegged, you do something that throws me." His voice sounded earnest and solemn. "I think I need to get to know you better."

"You seem to be accomplishing that rather quickly."

His tone became husky. "The more I discover, the more I want to know. We're not staying here long."

"Whatever you want," she answered softly, aware of a fluttering inside her.

He came around the car to take her arm and lead her in through the kitchen. Tath's simple bouquet of garden flowers no longer decorated the kitchen table. Instead, the oak table held dishes filled with tiny sandwiches, wedges of cheese, slices of ham, and iced cakes. After greeting two uniformed maids, Tath introduced them to Hilary. While they stood in the warm kitchen, which smelled of delicious food and hot coffee, Hilary glanced at the door to the utility room and felt a pang.

"Thinking of Snuffy?"

She looked up to find Tath watching her. "Yes, more than I thought I would. Where is he, Tath? I'd really like to visit him at the kennel," she said, suddenly remembering that she had been planning to ask Tath this question the first thing this evening.

"I'll tell you after the party," Tath promised. "In fact, I'll even guarantee that you'll get to see him again sooner than you think. Just trust me, Hilary."

Tath held her arm as they entered the dining room, which was filled with people standing and holding plates of food. Others moved around the table, serving themselves from platters of chicken and rice, cucumber mousse, green salad, fresh shrimp, and melons.

Tath greeted a dark-haired man whom he introduced to Hilary as Charles Donnley. Within a few minutes, more guests joined them. Behind her, Hilary heard a man say, "I'm Bob Fielding."

She turned around to face a dark-eyed man dressed in a gray suit. "May I get you a drink?" he asked.

She shook her head. "No, thank you. We just arrived." She glanced over her shoulder at Tath, who was talking to Charles Donnley and those standing beside him.

"Did you come with Tath?" Bob Fielding asked.

"Yes."

"There's some scrumptious food on that table. Tath may talk all night and you'll starve. Come on."

She smiled. "I'll wait a minute."

Her words faded as she heard Mrs. Justin join the group behind her. Her throaty voice carried clearly when she asked, "Tath, do you remember Mary Lynn Weber?"

"Hello, Mary Lynn," Tath said. Hilary felt a pang and wondered at herself.

Mrs. Justin continued, "Mary Lynn's planning a trip to

Mexico City, and I want you to tell her about the last time you were there."

Hilary turned to gaze at a tall blonde with a striking figure who spoke in a soft drawl while her blue eyes studied Tath. "I imagine you can tell me some of the exciting things to see."

He laughed. "Our ideas on what's exciting might not be the same, Mary Lynn." He reached out and put his arm around Hilary's waist. "Mother, you remember Hilary. Mary Lynn, this is Hilary O'Brien."

Hilary nodded at Mrs. Justin and saw the flash of cold gray eyes. Somehow, with Tath clasping her waist proprietarily, Mrs. Justin's venom failed to upset her. At that moment Greg Justin's voice boomed a greeting to everyone in general and he joined their cluster to speak to his mother.

Mrs. Justin said, "Greg, you're just the person we need. Why don't you show Miss O'Brien around, introduce her for Tath. Mary Lynn wanted to ask him some questions and I promised her he'd tell her about Mexico City."

"Sure thing," Greg said quickly, and took Hilary's arm. She glanced at Tath and saw him wink at her before she turned to walk away with Greg.

"I have a better idea than introducing you to all these people. Meeting forty people at once isn't my idea of fun. Come out here and let me show you Mother's flowers."

They moved across the room, down the hall away from the crowd. Hilary didn't particularly care to be alone with Greg, but Mrs. Justin's coldness and high-handed methods had nonplussed her. And if Tath wanted to talk to Mary Lynn Weber, she wasn't going to interfere.

As they strolled along the hall, a slender, black-haired woman emerged from a room along the upstairs hall. The moment she neared the steps and saw Greg, she called to him. "Greg!"

"Angie!" From the wide smile on Greg's face, Hilary guessed that he and Angie were well acquainted. She watched the woman rush down the stairs and into Greg's arms for a warm embrace. When he released her, he said, "Angie, I want you to meet Hilary O'Brien. Hilary, this is Angie Whitman, Miss Louisiana."

Angie Whitman laughed. "Don't tell her what year it was. I thought you'd call me."

"I didn't know you'd be home this soon."

Hilary patted his arm. "Greg, excuse me. I'll see you in a few minutes." She glanced at Angie and said, "It was nice to meet you."

Knowing Greg and Angie wouldn't miss her in the least, she strolled down the hall toward the back of the house. As she neared the empty music room, she heard Mrs. Justin's voice.

"I planned for you to escort Mary Lynn tonight, Tath, and you knew it! Instead you show up with . . . that woman whom I found you embracing in my kitchen this morning."

Hilary felt as if ice water had struck her. She halted and glanced over her shoulder to see if Angie and Greg had noticed her. While she waited in indecision about where to go, she heard Tath's calm voice.

"Mother, she isn't 'that woman,' she's Hilary O'Brien, and she's my date tonight."

"Oh, Tath! Mary Lynn is charming and from the finest family. Her great-granddaddy . . ."

Hilary turned quickly. She didn't want to hear any more. She could imagine every word, the words she had heard so many times from Blake's mother. For a moment she remembered the teas and parties during her engagement, when Mrs. Crowley would add to an introduction the same phrases about family and ancestry and finishing schools.

She reached Greg and Angie again. When he glanced at her, his eyes narrowed. "Hilary, are you all right?"

"I'm fine, Greg." She smiled and hurried past them to enter the living room, where she stood gazing at the milling guests. She realized Tath represented all the same things Blake had: wealth, a long-established line of ancestors who had put down roots long ago and flourished with the years. She thought of her own father, Michael O'Brien, a short, curly-haired barber who had moved too many times to count, a wandering man who was uncertain of the names of his ancestors only two generations removed.

"Miss O'Brien . . ."

Charles Donnley approached and asked her, "Care for a drink?"

"No, thank you."

"You're not from New Orleans?"

"No, I live in Dallas." While she explained her job and answered his questions, a couple joined them, and within a few more minutes others drifted up to form an ever-widening circle. The conversation changed and Hilary stood listening quietly while she wondered where Tath was. She glanced around and drew a sharp breath.

Only a few yards away, Tath stood in a group of men with one hand in his pocket. He was nodding while one of the men talked, but she knew he wasn't listening fully.

His gray eyes inched slowly over her black pumps, her sheer stockings, her black crepe dress, and she wished he'd stop because his gaze was like a caress. Every cell in her body responded, and a trail of warmth followed his look.

She wanted to turn away, yet at the same time she felt rooted to the floor, immobilized by the hungry, consuming fire in his eyes.

She licked her dry lips and watched him momentarily take his gaze from her while he spoke to the men. After a few seconds he stepped out of the group and strolled toward her. When he did, she felt her pulse jump. She turned to face the cluster of people around her, but she didn't hear a word Charles Donnley said. When Tath stopped directly behind her, his hand touched the small of her back.

One of the men in the group asked, "Did you see Kent Thompson the last time you were in New York, Tath?"

"No," he answered.

Another man nearby spoke. "I saw him, and he's opened an office in Miami, too . . ." The conversation ebbed and flowed around them while she felt Tath's fingers drawing circles on her spine. She knew he stood close enough that no one could see what he was doing.

It shouldn't mean anything, but it sent currents racing through her. She wanted to turn and put her arms around him, to hold him. She remembered his kisses and caresses and her quickened pulse beat even harder.

She felt his breath against her hair as he whispered, "Ready to go?"

She nodded and his hand dropped lightly on her waist. They drifted out of the circle and moved until they were standing alone. He paused and looked down at her. "Have you eaten dinner?"

She shook her head. The last thing she wanted was a plate of food. "Tath, get what you want. I'm not hungry."

His eyes narrowed and he tilted his head to look at her. "Mary Lynn Weber didn't get you down, did she?"

"No." She smiled at the thought. "I haven't lost my appetite because of her."

He continued to study her for a moment before he asked, "Was it Mother?" She looked into his eyes and he guessed her answer. "That shouldn't matter, Hilary," he said.

"It doesn't, much. Go get something to eat, Tath."

"Not without you. Hilary, why would you care what the hell Mother thinks?"

She glanced around. "Tath, this isn't the place to discuss your mother."

"Okay. Come eat a little."

She smiled and threw up her hands. "You win—as usual!"

- 10 -

AFTER SHE HAD eaten a dinner as delicious as Tath had promised, he introduced her to a few more people. They talked until finally he took her arm and headed for the kitchen.

Before they reached the back door, Mrs. Justin followed them into the kitchen and said, "Tath, surely you're not leaving."

He paused and turned to smile at his mother. "You have a house full of people to enjoy. You'll never miss us."

"You promised to come to this party."

"And I kept my promise. I'm here, Mother. Now enjoy your guests, I'm going to show Hilary my new houseboat."

Mrs. Justin closed her eyes momentarily. "Oh, Tath! It's ridiculous to live on a boat! Miss O'Connor won't mind if you stay."

"It's O'Brien, Mother, Hilary O'Brien," he said quietly.

Mrs. Justin looked at Hilary for the first time since she'd entered the kitchen. "My dear, I'm sorry. Miss O'Brien, you don't mind staying here a little longer, do you?"

Tath laughed. "Don't prevail on Hilary's good nature." He put his arm around her shoulders. "We've had a nice time, Mother, and now we're going."

"The food was delicious, Mrs. Justin," Hilary remarked.

Tath leaned forward to kiss his mother on the cheek. "I'll be over tomorrow." He took Hilary's arm, and together they turned toward the door as someone called for Mrs. Justin from the dining room.

When they stepped outside, the night air was cool; beneath a clear, starry sky, wide-spreading trees cast long shadows in the moonlight. Once they had driven away, Hilary said, "Your mother expected you to spend the evening with Mary Lynn."

Tath lit a cigarette and grinned at her. "This is better."

She settled in the seat while he drove through suburban areas until they left the city behind.

Houses thinned, spreading farther and farther apart. The air became cooler, whipping in through the open window as Tath sped along. Dark clumps of trees bordered the highway, and Hilary enjoyed the silence. When Tath slowed to turn onto a country road, she glanced at him.

"We're on a back road, but this is my property and the boat is anchored here. I want you to see it and I have a surprise for you."

The Porsche skidded and slid in the muddy road. She looked at him intently. "A surprise?"

"You'll see soon enough." High grass and live oaks lined the narrow road, which curved and became more muddy. They rounded another bend, and ahead Hilary saw the river beyond the levee. A white wooden dock stretched into the Mississippi, with a houseboat anchored at the end of the dock. Moonlight sent a shimmering white reflection across the dark waters of the river, and the moment Tath turned off the car motor, Hilary heard frogs croaking, the shrill chirping of crickets, and the rhythmical lapping of water against pilings.

He came around and opened the door for her, his arm snaking around her waist and hugging her to him as they walked. They were alone, the night was cool, the river looked beautiful, and she was keenly aware of Tath's arm around her, the smells of his fresh cotton shirt and his aftershave, the warmth of his body. Their feet clattered as they stepped onto the wooden dock.

Suddenly another sound startled her. A series of barks erupted and she looked at Tath in astonishment as she recognized the familiar sound of the wild barking.

"That's the surprise!" He grinned. "I knew you didn't really want to put Snuffy in a kennel." He took her hand to walk the last few steps before they crossed a plank to his houseboat.

Snuffy bounded forward to meet them and Hilary knelt to scoop him up and give him a squeeze. Overjoyed to have the wriggling, fuzzy dog, she laughed and looked up at Tath.

"As bad as he is, I'm glad to see him again. I've been feeling guilty all day about not visiting him." She stood up and Snuffy twisted to reach Tath, who scratched his head. "Thanks, Tath." She stood on tiptoe and kissed his cheek.

He smiled. "You're welcome."

She glanced around. "You gave him the run of the boat. He may have chewed up something."

He reached out to take Snuffy from her arms. "No, look at old Snuffy. He's a natural sailor and he loves the water. Watch him run up where he can look over the side." He set Snuffy down. The terrier sat down at Tath's feet, looked up expectantly, and wagged his tail.

She laughed. "I can see how much he loves this boat."

"That mutt does have an ornery streak," Tath remarked dryly. "Come on, let me show you my new quarters."

As he took her arm, Hilary glanced around. "This is hardly what I envisioned when you said you had a houseboat."

"It's a yacht, but it's a houseboat for me. It's a fifty-six-footer with an eighteen-foot beam, and I love it."

While he talked, they descended to a lounge filled with white and blue furnishings. Tath stepped behind a bar, where he opened a bottle of champagne, poured two glasses, and handed one to Hilary.

"Here's to Snuffy."

She raised her glass. "Thanks again."

"At least until his next escapade," Tath added, touching her glass with his and taking a sip. While they drank, Snuffy perched happily in a chair nearby. Tath took Hilary's hand. "Let's take this topside. It'll be nice on deck." As they left, he shut Snuffy behind in the lounge.

When he did, Hilary murmured, "That's risky."

"Snuffy and I have an understanding."

"I'll remind you of that when he's torn up some of those pretty blue cushions."

Tath led her up to the bridge deck, pulled out a cushioned chair, and motioned to her. As soon as she sat down, he said, "I'll be with you shortly."

Enjoying the cool air and the river, she sipped her champagne. The hum of diesel engines commenced, drowning out the noises of frogs and insects. In a few minutes she felt the gentle movement of the yacht as it began to edge away from the dock.

She settled back in the chair to gaze high overhead at bright stars and the cold, white moon that bathed the world in its silvery light.

As they moved upriver, she looked at the dark oaks lining the banks. With each breeze, delicate tendrils of Spanish moss swayed above the water. The yacht changed direction slightly and headed closer to the bank. The engines died and silence descended. River sounds surfaced again, a bird's melodic night cry and bullfrogs' deep constant croaking.

"Like it here?"

Tath moved soundlessly beside her. He held an icebucket containing the bottle of champagne and his glass. He placed the bucket on deck and refilled her glass, then he waved his hand, motioning her to move over. "There's room for both of us."

For an instant she hesitated. If he sat that close, she would be in his arms. She gazed up at him and moved over.

He seemed to fill the chair. Through his fine cotton shirt, his body was warm. He shifted her so that she sat in the crook of his shoulder with his arm around her, his fingers curving lightly against her bare arm.

She was aware of the length of him pressed against her, his hipbone, the long legs, the faint odor of tobacco on his clothing.

He sighed with contentment. "I love it on the water. That damned mill really gets to me."

"It is pretty here. I've never been around boats or on them that much, particularly since I don't swim."

"You don't know what you've missed, Hilary. This is almost perfect."

"What's needed to make it perfect?" He'd distracted her with his talk about boats, the mill, and the river. Too late, she realized she'd risen fully to his opening gambit as he turned slightly and drew her more tightly to him.

His voice was throaty when he said, "It's getting closer to perfection." He turned her face toward his and took the champagne from her hand to place it on the deck.

"Tath, I meant what I said in the car." She struggled to keep her voice normal, but it was difficult with his mouth only inches away and his smoky eyes devouring her with a hunger that set her tingling inside. "You may not see yourself as a sheik, but—"

"Hilary, relax," he said huskily. "Nothing will happen unless you want it to."

She looked at him to gauge his sincerity, but she couldn't fathom his feelings any more than she could discern what lay beneath the river's dark surface. "A few kisses doesn't have to lead to anything," he coaxed.

She smiled. "Tath, I can't imagine you've had a relationship like that with any woman for a long time now."

He still continued to look at her closely. "There really isn't any harem, Hilary."

"Oh, no. There's just Meredith and Gloria and Natalie, and probably Mary Lynn Weber if she gets the chance, and . . ."

"Don't tell me you haven't even kissed anyone since Blake."

She felt a twinge of aggravation. "Yes, I have, but they weren't . . ." She bit off the words instantly.

"Weren't what?" His insistent voice was velvety.

"Are you fishing for compliments?"

He turned slightly and his arm tightened around her waist while he reached up to twist a coppery curl around his finger. "I damn well might be. They weren't what?" he asked again.

"They weren't so disturbing or exciting," she said, "and that makes this all the more dangerous."

In the distance a ship's horn blew a rumbling bass note,

followed by a bird's soft cry. Near the boat, something splashed, but with her attention on the magnetic man beside her, Hilary barely heard any of the sounds.

"You're not going to get hurt," he whispered. "You won't fall in love, because you've already told me that I'm dictatorial." He tilted his head to one side and leaned down to brush her neck lightly with his lips.

"I'm egotistical," he went on, as his warm lips trailed along her throat to her shoulder. "Let's see . . . I'm also nice . . ." She felt another moist kiss on her neck. "And I'm disturbing . . ."

She closed her eyes and whispered, "You certainly are." It was the most natural thing in the world to turn her mouth to his. His lips captured hers, and his tongue invaded her mouth. She felt an explosive burst of warmth at her core.

He lifted her to his lap and she wound her arms around his neck. With a shuddering sigh, she pulled his head closer, arching against him as she felt his hand move down the length of her.

Responding, she pressed against him, returning his fiery, probing kisses. Passion exploded; the need for more of Tath, for greater intimacy with him, filled her.

Her eyes opened and she gazed at his long, thick eyelashes, the fine web of lines around the corners of his eyes. He raised his head and looked at her, and she wondered how deeply involved her feelings were.

With a quick movement he lowered the back of the chair until it was horizontal. He shifted and lay on his side to pull her into his arms.

Even while she returned his kisses, she knew she should guard against loving him. He would never return her love; to Tath, she would be only one of the many women in his life. She was surprised by the stab of pain this thought caused her. But the pang was brief, swept away by the intense sensations that flooded her as he caressed her.

His hands became something apart, a fluid, sensuous touch that destroyed reason.

She felt his fingers on the row of buttons that ran from the neck to the waist of her black crepe dress. The air was cool against her skin, his fingertips warm as they brushed her back.

He kissed her shoulder, pushing the soft crepe away, tugging it to her waist. "What lovely skin you have, Hilary, and your breasts . . ." he murmured, his voice hoarse with urgency. He brought his burning lips first to one nipple, then the other, searing her innermost being as the rosy buds grew rigid with desire.

Abruptly he sat up and unbuttoned his shirt, peeling it off his bronzed shoulders and letting it fall to the deck.

For an instant she gazed at his hard, tough body and wondered how it could be so important to her, so necessary. Why could he do what others couldn't? Why did he have such power to stir her? She gazed up at him, the broad shoulders, the chest covered with dark hair, and reached up to touch him lightly with her fingertips.

He caught her hand and kissed her fingers, turning her palm while he watched her with calm eyes. With fluid ease, he stretched beside her to slip an arm beneath her waist and pull her close and kiss her languorously.

Within seconds, any resistance, any hesitation, was lost forever, driven away by his expert caresses, his tormenting kisses. Gently, with tenderness, he melted her reserve. The remainder of her clothes dropped to the deck. His were flung aside until there was no hindrance, nothing between them. Her body pressed against his, their legs entwined, then he lifted his head to gaze down at her.

His eyes were dark, unreadable, and piercing, while he looked at her a moment in silence before leaning forward to kiss her hungrily. When at last he released her mouth, he whispered softly, "What a desirable woman you are, Hilary. How much I want you . . ."

With silken caresses, he drove her to wanton abandon. She cherished his hard male body, thrilling to his touch, his butterfly kisses on her forehead, her throat, the valley between her breasts.

It was impossible to talk as he stroked her lightly. Her teeth caught her lower lip for a moment before she gasped with pleasure.

Her fingers explored, evoking as deep a response from him as he did from her. She felt his heart thudding against hers; his breathing was ragged and heavy. She knew that physically he experienced as much unbearable, hungry passion as she. Emotionally, there was a difference.

She loved him. Hopelessly, impossibly, but the love she felt for him couldn't be denied. She groaned and pulled his mouth to hers to kiss him fiercely.

When she did, his arms crushed her against him while he returned the kiss with unrelenting insistence.

He turned his head and as his hands traveled over her slender body, he whispered, "I've never known anyone like you, Hilary. I need you..."

She couldn't comprehend what he said. She was lost like bubbles in a whirlpool, drawn down into a vortex of passion. She was beyond words. Molten desire burned through her veins and she clung to him, melting into his tough, brown body as his legs shifted between hers.

"Hilary. My own darling Hilary. How I want to love you... let me love you."

"Oh, Tath. Yes..." With a low moan, she gave herself to him utterly, completely, with no holding back. Another cry escaped her lips. It was a cry of ecstasy, of love, of joy, as all desire rose, and crashed to fulfillment.

For an instant she felt as if she were a part of him. She felt complete, whole. His arms tightened and he shifted to his side to pull her close and kiss her deeply.

He relaxed slightly and looked at her, and she felt as if she might melt beneath the warmth in his gaze. "You're very special, Hilary."

Clarity and reason returned as swiftly as they had gone, and she no longer wanted to declare the feelings that welled up inside her. She loved him, but the words couldn't be said when she knew they would be meaningless to him. She gazed at him intently, watching him smile and reach out to brush her hair away from her face.

He kissed her cheek and whispered, "You're the most beautiful woman in the universe." He kissed her ear lightly. "And the sexiest..."

She laughed. "And you're too full of compliments to be believed!"

He chuckled softly. "I like your smile. I meant every word. This is perfection—absolute and complete."

"I thought roaming around the South Pole, chasing penguins and whales, was your idea of perfection," she whispered, and traced her finger across his hard cheekbone.

She heard the amusement in his voice. "That runs a close second to this."

"Thanks, I'm highly flattered to know that I win out over penguins."

With mock solemnity, he said, "Of course you do! You're rounder here than a penguin..." His fingers brushed her shoulder. "You're a bit smaller in the middle." His fingers drifted across her skin to her waist and she caught his hand to lock her fingers in his.

"That's enough! I get your point. You'll start something again."

He laughed softly and settled on his back, pulling her into the crook of his shoulder. "Look at that sky."

She turned and gazed overhead at endless twinkling stars. "It looks like several thousand more popped out since we left the city," he said.

They looked up silently. Water lapped against the boat and Hilary felt a slight rocking motion. She was conscious of his bare flesh against hers, his arms around her, his sinewy forearms beneath her hands. It *was* perfection, she thought, and a nagging reminder came that it was very temporary. She shoved away the thought and looked at the white moon high above. She sighed. "It's beautiful."

His fingertips trailed the length of her body and his voice sounded awed. "Beyond all belief."

He propped himself up on an elbow to gaze at her. Hilary lay still beneath his scrutiny. Deep inside she felt a flare of smoldering passion, a deep need for Tath. It spread through her as his gaze assessed her with a devouring look.

His voice deepened. "You're so very beautiful, Hilary." She placed her hand against his chest and felt his quickened heartbeat. He caught her up in his arms and kissed her as hungrily as if it were the first time.

How easy to wrap her arms around his neck and return his kiss, to start again the torment that blazed with ravenous fire.

Later, near dawn, she finally slept in his arms while the yacht bobbed on the wide Mississippi River.

During the early morning hours, Tath drove her to the Hotel St. Jean where she changed into a conservative navy blue dress and pumps. She combed her hair and leaned forward to study her reflection in the mirror, thinking she didn't look any different, yet she had changed. It didn't show, but she would never again be the same person she had been before she met Tath. She didn't know how deep her feelings went, but she knew they were more solid than what she had felt for Blake. *Disaster*. The word raced through her mind, and she put it away resolutely. She would spend the day with Tath, and right now that was all that mattered.

- 11 -

SHE MET TATH in the lobby of the hotel and they drove to the mill. It was too early for anyone else to be there, she thought as they entered the darkened building. The moment Tath opened the door, the musty, dank smell of mildew struck them. He held the door, following her inside and turning on the lights.

"I'll get some windows open and the fan going. This won't smell so bad when it's aired out. Most of our employees will be in today. Let's go down to my office and I'll get some things out of the way before we start our tour. How's that?"

"Fine."

He laughed softly and caught her wrist to pull her into his arms. "Fine," he repeated. He smiled while he held her. "This morning everything's great!" He kissed her lightly. "You're delightful, Hilary O'Brien."

She smiled at him. "And you're devastating, Tath Justin."

He leaned down and kissed her, this time deeply, driving away all awareness of her surroundings, setting her heart pounding and making her kiss him fiercely in return.

He released her and gazed down at her intently. "I'm ready to head back to the boat."

"They'd just call you to come down here," she remarked, and he released her with a smile, keeping his arm around her shoulders to walk to his office.

Turning on lights and moving through the front office, he opened his door and pulled a chair in front of his desk for Hilary.

She sat down and watched while he moved around the room, getting papers out of the desk, studying a note pad. He rose and headed toward the outer office. "I need something from the files. Kitty should be here by now."

Hilary watched as he strolled through the door. With his back to her, he stood at the filing cabinet. His dark hair curled thickly above his tan neck.

When she looked at his white shirt tapering from his broad shoulders to his slim waist, she thought of the taut muscles, the smooth skin she'd explored only hours ago.

Clicking high heels sounded in the hall and in seconds she heard a high, breathless female voice greet Tath.

"Good morning! I waited for you . . ."

A petite blonde in a red jersey dress came into view, walking to Tath without hesitation. She put her arms around him and kissed him.

A cold shock rippled through Hilary, followed instantly by the wry knowledge that what she saw was nothing new. She didn't like it. It hurt more than she would have guessed, and she realized again how strong were the feelings Tath evoked in her.

He disentangled himself from the woman's arms and said, "Kitty, there's . . ."

"You said you might pick me up for breakfast this morning, remember?"

"Sorry, Kitty, something came up."

He took her arm and spoke forcefully. "Kitty, there's someone here I want you to meet."

Hilary crossed her legs and faced Tath and the woman as they entered the office. "Hilary, this is my secretary, Kitty Rogers. Kitty, this is Miss O'Brien, who's here from Visual Communications in Dallas."

Hilary smiled and said hello, while Kitty's blue eyes grew round and she blushed deeply. She looked up at Tath, whose face was flushed. "I'm sorry, Tath, I didn't know anyone was here."

"That's all right. Would you get the folder on the Cooper order?"

"Yes, sir." She turned and left, and Tath closed the door.

"I'm sorry that happened," he said. "It doesn't mean anything."

Hilary attempted a laugh, though inside she was churning with pain. Did *she* mean anything to him, beyond the transient pleasure of their lovemaking? "You look as guilty as sin, Tath. It doesn't matter. There weren't any strings tied on you last night."

She saw a flash of surprise in his eyes. She hoped that what she felt deep inside didn't show and that her voice sounded casual.

He didn't move, but stood at the door studying her. "Is something wrong?" she asked.

He frowned. "Well, hell! I'd like you to sound even faintly miffed." He waved toward the door. "Don't you give a damn if I kiss Kitty or if I date Kitty or if I never ask you out again?"

Before she could answer, he snapped, "And don't give me any baloney about baldheaded, thirty-eight-year-old Blake! You really don't care what I do?"

"Tath, last night was wonderful, but I just said there weren't any strings—not on you or on me. Right?"

"That's right," he answered warily, "we didn't make any commitments. I can't make any, but that doesn't mean I take it so lightly I don't give a damn whom you kiss."

She laughed. "That's ridiculous, Tath! Either there are strings attached or there aren't—it isn't a halfway proposition."

He studied her intently and mumbled, "I never can tell with you."

"Tell what?"

"What's going on in that mind of yours," he answered flatly, and crossed to his desk. "I thought you didn't like me, that you weren't the least interested, even disliked me— and I found out that wasn't the case at all. Now you act so supremely indifferent, I can't help but wonder if you're at it again." His eyes narrowed. "Suppose I cancel my lunch date with you and go out with Kitty instead. Wouldn't that aggravate you?"

Hilary shrugged. "Tomorrow I go home to Dallas to get

a proposal ready for you. When I'm gone you'll ask Kitty to lunch, or Meredith, or some other woman, so it isn't the end of the world if it comes a day sooner."

His eyes flashed and a muscle worked in his jaw as he leaned across the desk to look at her. "I clearly recall a statement from you that you don't believe in bed-hopping. If you take last night that lightly . . ."

She laughed. "Tath, lower your voice! I don't care to have your secretary hear this conversation!" Deep inside she felt a degree of satisfaction. He'd already caused her grief, and it looked as if he would cause her a great deal more. She didn't want to be another Meredith or Kitty to him. His annoyance was flattering.

He compressed his lips a moment. In a swift movement he came around the desk and reached down to pull her to her feet. His eyes were intent and probing, searching hers. "How many other men are there in your life right now, Hilary?"

She smiled and smoothed his tie. "Tath, that's none of your business. At this moment there's only one—you— but what difference does it make?"

His eyes darkened and his brows drew together. In silence he looked down at her and she felt her pulse quicken. His gaze lowered to her mouth and he pulled her into his arms to kiss her.

It was a kiss that consumed her. Possessively, intimately, his deep, thorough plundering of her mouth claimed her as much as the consummation the night before. After the first breathless moment, she wrapped her arms around his neck and stood on tiptoe to respond to his fierce demand.

His raging need spread warmth through her, unleashing a returning ardor, a quivering longing. She pushed against him.

"We might get interrupted at any minute."

"Hilary, you have a damned casual attitude for someone who seemed very earnest last night."

She looked up and answered quietly, "I *was* earnest last night."

"What do you feel for me now?"

She smiled, placing her hands on his shoulders. "What do you feel for *me*, Tath?"

Suddenly he laughed. "You're getting me so mixed up, I don't know what I feel! This conversation isn't getting me anywhere." His hands fell away and he walked around his desk to sit down.

Hilary settled in the chair again and crossed her legs. "Don't worry about it, Tath. Most men would be thankful. And look at Kitty. She didn't seem upset at meeting me, yet it should be obvious to her that I'm the reason you forgot your breakfast date with her."

He moved to the desk. "Oh, well, it means nothing with Kitty."

"And I'm different?" She hated herself for fishing like that, but couldn't seem to help it.

He looked at her darkly. "I'll be ready to look at the mill in a few minutes. It's about time everyone started work."

A buzz interrupted him and he pressed the intercom button. Hilary heard Kitty say, "Mrs. Justin is on the phone."

"Thanks." Tath picked up the phone. While he said hello, Hilary looked down at her purse. As she brushed the lint off it, she heard Tath say, "I'll be there. I'll meet you and Elliot at quarter past twelve. No, I won't be alone. Hilary will be with me."

She glanced up at him and met his gaze. He swung the chair around and faced the wall, with his profile to her.

"Hilary, Mother—Miss O'Brien. She was with me last night."

Hilary could imagine the other end of the conversation. Mrs. Justin refused to acknowledge her existence, it seemed. She heard Tath say, "Hilary's with me right now, and we'll both be there at twelve-fifteen."

Hilary knew it wouldn't do any good to interrupt him and tell him to go without her, so she waited quietly. When she saw a flush creep up his cheek, she guessed his mother was arguing and she suspected she was the cause of Mrs. Justin's querulousness.

Tath asked lightly, "Mother, do you want me there? Fine. Hilary and I will see you later, then." He replaced the receiver and turned to look at Hilary.

"I don't have to eat lunch with you, you know," she said.

"Pay no attention to that. We're having our photograph taken. Mother's birthday is coming up soon and she wanted to commemorate the event with a family picture. The photographer will be at her house around noon, and Greg and I have to be there. It won't take long, and we'll eat lunch with her." He tilted his head to one side and held up his hand in a helpless gesture. "I'm sorry. I'd rather be alone with you, but I promised this long ago."

"That's fine, but I wish you'd go without me."

"Absolutely out of the question."

Somewhere in the mill a whistle blew, and Tath glanced at his watch. He rose and moved around the desk. "Shall we start?"

Tath held her arm until they halted in front of Kitty's desk. "We'll be in the mill," he said.

Kitty's blue eyes narrowed as she looked at Hilary, who smiled and turned to catch Tath watching her. Once they were in the hall, he remained quiet until they reached the large room filled with machinery. Light streamed down from overhead and the room was filled with the clatter and hum of engines. Tath paused beside a large, round machine. While Hilary made notes and watched bales of cotton rotate, Tath explained, "This is an opener-picker machine, which loosens, cleans, and blends the fibers."

She watched bales revolve over beaters that pulled apart the cotton. Next they watched the fibers roll between large cylinders. Tath said, "This is the carding, where fibers are straightened."

Hilary jotted down a notation and looked at him. "When the yarn comes out here, do you still have loose fibers?"

"These will be slivers called carded yarns. After this will come the drawing operation, and roving, where the fibers are blended and drawn out until they're suitable for spinning."

As they strolled along, people dressed in brown denims worked quietly, speaking to Tath. He called everyone by his or her first name, and stopped to chat for a moment with several employees, raising his voice above the clatter of machinery.

In front of the spinning machines, Hilary sketched quickly, developing a rough drawing while long rows of spindles whirled, winding up yarn. Tath showed her the dyeing process and printmaking. Finally they finished and returned to the hall. "Do you think you have enough information?" he asked.

She looked down at her notes. "More than enough."

"Good. It's time to eat lunch. I'll step into the office and tell Kitty where I'll be, and then we'll go."

Hilary was not looking forward to having lunch with Mrs. Justin. She watched Tath stroll down the hall with his shoulders straight, his long legs moving in an easy stride. In a few minutes he returned. As he approached, his gaze traveled with an exaggerated, mocking leer from her head to her toes.

Hilary laughed. "I take it you approve of my outfit."

He put his arm around her. "Not one bit. It gets in my way. I was imagining your..."

"Tath!" she interrupted him."For heaven's sake! Someone will hear you."

He held the door and they emerged into bright sunshine and climbed into his car. Tath drove out of the parking lot and down the street past warehouses. Suddenly he whipped into a deserted alley and turned off the ignition.

"What are you doing?"

He turned to pull her into his arms. "Hilary, I can't wait any longer. I have an irresistible urge..."

She laughed. "You're crazy!"

His lips stopped her conversation as he pulled her to him. The kiss was tantalizing, passionate, and brief—because she pushed him away.

Smiling, she said, "I'll look rumpled when I have lunch with your mother."

"I couldn't resist." He moved beneath the steering wheel again and drove to his house to park and enter through the kitchen door. Hilary dreaded the encounter with his mother because she knew her presence wasn't welcome to Mrs. Justin.

Her feelings didn't change when they met Greg, Elliot Compton, and Tath's mother in the library, where the photographer had set up his equipment. Mrs. Justin's eyes narrowed and she studied Hilary intently. A flutter went through Hilary. She felt as if her stockings had just developed runs, her slip showed, and her hair needed combing, but she smiled and tried to sound composed as she said, "Hello, Mrs. Justin."

"Hello, Miss O'Brien. You're late, Tath, and Mr. Franklin is waiting."

"I was delayed, Mother, and we're about two minutes late." Tath stepped forward and introduced himself and Hilary to the photographer. While Mr. Franklin seated the family, Hilary crossed to sit in a chair beside Elliot Compton.

Elliot shifted toward her and asked, "How are you coming with your commercials?"

"Fine," she answered. "I just toured the mill and I have enough to do the storyboard and work up a budget."

"Good. And how's your little dog?"

"He's fine. He's on Tath's houseboat."

Elliot's eyebrows rose. "Oh? Wonderful!" His voice was filled with satisfaction. "You and Tath must be getting along just dandy."

She remembered Tath's statement that both his mother and Elliot wanted him to marry. Elliot was making it obvious that Hilary was his candidate. Hilary sighed. It only showed how little he knew about Tath. He wasn't about to ask her to marry him. She looked at the three Justins sitting on the sofa—Greg, Tath, and their mother. The brothers were handsome men, and Mrs. Justin was unusually attractive. They looked immaculately dressed, poised, and self-assured.

The photographer snapped the picture. Tath's gaze shifted, and he winked at Hilary. She smiled and felt a stir of warmth inside. Beside her, Elliot let out his breath in a sigh, and she wondered if he'd noticed Tath's wink. She looked into the comptroller's bright blue eyes and he smiled.

As soon as the pictures were over, Greg told them good-bye, saying he had an appointment. After he left, they strolled to the dining room, to a table set with gleaming crystal and sterling flatwear on a white linen tablecloth. A bouquet of red roses and white carnations in a crystal vase graced the center of the table. Tath held Hilary's chair as Elliot assisted Mrs. Justin, and they sat down to lunch.

While the maid served chilled chicken salad with white grapes and slivered almonds on crisp green lettuce, Mrs. Justin glanced at Hilary and asked, "Where are you from, Miss O'Brien?"

"Dallas."

"She's with Visual Communications, Mother," Tath explained. "I told you, they're doing the commercials for us."

"How nice. What does your father do, Miss O'Brien?"

"He's a barber."

"Oh?" Mrs. Justin's chin rose slightly and she gazed at Hilary. "I see." She looked at her son. "Tath, I do want you to attend the Power's party next week. I know you're invited. It's Saturday night."

Hilary felt as if she'd been scrutinized and dismissed by Tath's mother. A barber's daughter was obviously no match for a Justin. It shouldn't rankle, but it did. She only hoped it didn't show. She listened as Tath answered, "I already have plans, Mother."

Hilary remembered Blake's mother asking questions about her background. She was certain Mrs. Justin had stopped quizzing her because she wasn't interested in the women who were only temporarily part of Tath's life.

While the conversation continued, Hilary looked at the frilly white carnations and red roses in the centerpiece. She wondered which woman Tath would take out Saturday night. Meredith? Gloria? What did it matter, Hilary chided herself. She would be back in Dallas. Her attention shifted to the conversation as Mrs. Justin said, "Tath, you'll have to get your tuxedo cleaned for the Arts Ball."

He smiled. "I won't come in a dirty tux, Mother."

Elliot laughed and Mrs. Justin frowned. "Don't encourage him, Elliot."

Still chuckling, Elliot looked at Tath. "Did you find the files on the Cooper order?"

"Yes, Kitty has them ready for you."

The talk moved to business at the mill, some family friends Hilary didn't know, and the new cook at the country club. Finally there was a lull in the conversation, and Hilary saw Mrs. Justin give Elliot a significant look. Elliot placed his fork on his plate, coughed, and reached into an inner pocket of his jacket. He withdrew a slip of paper that could only be a check, and passed it wordlessly to Tath, who took it with an inquiring look at his mother.

Mrs. Justin met his gaze steadily, then shifted her attention to Hilary. "Miss O'Brien, I'm sorry if we must go into personal matters now. I told Tath I wanted to see him alone for lunch, but he refused to come without you."

Hilary blushed and wished Tath had not insisted that she accompany him. She glanced at him, expecting him to speak up, but he held the check in his hand and his eyes were narrowed as he studied it. He looked over the check at his mother.

"This is extremely generous, Mother. Unbelievably so."

Mrs. Justin looked again at Elliot before meeting her son's eyes. "That's a gift for your exploration people."

Tath straightened and looked at her intently. "What prompted this generosity?"

Again Mrs. Justin glanced at Hilary. "This is a little difficult under the circumstances."

Hilary started to push back her chair, but Tath caught her hand. "Go ahead, Mother."

Mrs. Justin looked at Tath's hand on Hilary's arm. She faced Hilary. "You needn't leave, my dear. Just please excuse our discussing something so personal before you." She turned to her son and said, "Tath, I'm making this gift to your organization in compensation for your services. If you'll settle down, take over the mill, marry if you want, this money goes to that organization."

Tath looked at the check in silence. Mrs. Justin continued, "As you can see, it's a very liberal donation. So much so that they might prefer it to your services."

Hilary looked at Tath. There wasn't a flicker of expression in his gray eyes. She couldn't guess what was in his thoughts, or what his reaction to his mother's proposition might be.

Mrs. Justin spoke quickly. "Don't decide hastily, Tath. I know this will make you angry, but we need you at the mill. You can run it and you're old enough to settle down. This gallivanting to the ends of the earth is ridiculous! I've notified the organization of my offer."

Tath looked at Elliot Compton. "No doubt this would be a nice write-off at tax time."

Elliot smiled. "Indeed it would. You'd have an excellent salary, Tath. I've been over that with you before. You'd have stock options, insurance, all the standard benefits. We need you, your creativity and your brains. Your father would want you to do this."

Tath let the check float to the table and Hilary glanced down at it. It was easy to see the staggering sum neatly penned on the face of the check. She raised her head and looked at Tath, and a sudden rush of sympathy surged through her. A silent voice inside her prayed that he would refuse to acquiesce in his mother's plans.

Why should he give up his hopes and dreams, the work he enjoyed, when Madeline Justin could hire someone who wanted the job to run Justin Mills? Hilary wound her fingers together and looked at Tath. With all her being, she wished he could say no, resist the efforts of his mother and Elliot to run his life, make his decisions for him.

Tath picked up the check again. When he did, Mrs. Justin smiled and lifted her fork to take a bite. "Think about it, Tath. We're in no great hurry. This is a big decision and it must be right for you, but, darling, how could you go wrong at the mill?"

Elliot added, "Remember, too, that if you go to the South Pole, we'll have to find someone to take over for you. You won't have an offer like this again, Tath."

"I know," Tath replied, and Hilary longed to reach over and touch him, to tell him to determine his own priorites.

Elliot reached into his coat pocket and produced another check, which he placed in front of Tath. "If you accept our offer here's your first month's pay. You'll have an increase over what you make now."

Again Hilary could see the amount and it was as staggering as the first check. Tath frowned and raised his head to look at Elliot. "You can't afford to pay me such a high salary."

Both Elliot and Mrs. Justin smiled as Elliot answered, "Indeed we can. You've increased business sufficiently this year that the board knows how valuable you'll be."

Once again, Hilary had a glimpse of the steel behind Elliot's baby-blue eyes when his voice hardened. "You can't make that salary anywhere else, Tath. You never will in oceanography."

Mrs. Justin touched her son's hand. "Tath, this is absolutely right for you. You're perfect for the job, and your father would be so proud of you."

Elliot leaned forward. "Tath, you know you've stepped into your father's shoes without effort. You're a natural at running a business like Justin Mills. You've grown up with it and you know every aspect, from the farms to the customers who buy the fabric. Someday you'd have to give up these explorations anyway—that day will just come a little sooner."

He paused, and Tath glanced at him, but didn't say a word. Undaunted, Elliot continued, "It doesn't mean you can't travel or take short expeditions—or even retire early and devote yourself to oceanography then."

"I'll have to give it some thought, Elliot."

Hilary saw the quick, triumphant glance Madeline Justin sent Elliot Compton. Mrs. Justin said, "Good, Tath, that's all we ask."

Tath sat back and picked up the check Elliot had given him. "I have to hand it to both of you. If I accept, you'll get what you want and a healthy tax deduction to boot."

Elliot smiled. "Take your time, Tath. We want you to

be certain of your decision. Keep the checks. If you decide against this, you can tell me and destroy them."

Tath picked up both checks and put them in his coat pocket while his mother said, "Elliot, when we finish lunch, remind me to call the florist. I need to see about flowers."

The polite inconsequential chatter that followed was difficult and Hilary was relieved when Tath rose and took her hand. She echoed his good-byes to his mother and Elliot.

Once they were in the car, headed away from the house, Tath said, "Sorry you had to be in on that scene."

"That's all right."

"They've really put the squeeze on me this time. I know what the exploration people would prefer."

Hilary's heart ached at the bitterness in his voice. "Are you sure you're not underestimating your abilities?" she asked softly.

"How do you know that they wouldn't prefer the check?" he asked in reply.

"I don't think this would be such a difficult decision for you if you didn't think they'd like the donation more."

"You're right. I'm sorry you were embroiled in Elliot's and Mother's dealings."

"Don't worry about me. You won't let your mother and Elliot push you into something you don't like, will you?"

"I'll try not to," he answered lightly, but she wondered if he could withstand the kind of pressure they had exerted.

He slowed the car and stopped in front of the hotel. Smiling, he said, "I'll be by to get you about seven."

He slipped his hand behind her neck and pulled her forward to kiss her before he opened the door. She stepped out and crossed the walk to enter the hotel. She was aware of the roar of Tath's car as he drove away and had to fight the urge to watch him drive out of sight.

- *12* -

WHEN SHE REACHED her room, Hilary paused and gazed at the soft blue decorations, the smooth walnut headboard, and the bright oil paintings on the wall. She changed into jeans and a knit shirt before getting out her notes and sitting down at the desk to go to work.

Spreading her notes on the desktop, she sketched panels showing each shot for the commercials.

After a time, she reached for the phone directory to look up some numbers, which she jotted down. She began to place calls to get approximate figures on how high the costs would run for various scenes, for hiring staff, for renting a helicopter, and for acquiring props for one of the scenes.

She thought about Tath and the previous night on his boat, and everything inside her seemed to turn to quivering jelly. She laid her pencil on the papers and stared into space, filled with longing and trembling excitement.

Working diligently, she forced her thoughts back to the task at hand until she saw that it was almost time for Tath to pick her up. She was so close to getting a rough storyboard put together for him that she continued to sketch. It would be easier if she could get his comments on her ideas before she left for Dallas.

Concentrating all her efforts, she leaned over the papers and worked until she ran short of time. Finally she rushed to take a bath, but before she finished dressing, she heard a rap on the door of her room.

She stepped into a pale green cotton dress, pulled the zipper up the back, and hurried in her stocking feet to the door.

"Hilary?" She heard Tath's familiar voice as she unlocked and opened the door.

The first hill on a roller coaster couldn't have caused her insides to flutter more than they did as she faced him. She hoped her nervousness didn't show as she smiled and stepped to one side. His white shirt made him appear darkly handsome, and his trim gray slacks were impeccable. "Tath, I'm sorry I'm late. I was working on the storyboard and I lost track of time."

He laughed. "You never let up, do you?"

She tilted her head to look at him and he drawled, "It's disconcerting to find that your work is more intriguing than our date."

"I didn't mean that at all."

"Of course not!" he answered breezily, but she noticed that he was watching her intently.

"Come look at this." She moved to the desk and pulled another chair close to hers. Tath sat down and took the storyboard in one hand to turn the pages slowly.

"Here's a shot of the cotton field from above... The camera can be mounted on a helicopter so it won't bounce around. It'll be right outside the door. We'll zoom in on the first shot of cotton; next we'll be high above—with a long shot of cotton fields bordered by live oaks."

She turned a page to show him another sketch. "We'll move to just outside the mill, again with a shot from above. Then we'll go inside with a scene showing one of the machines..."

He smiled at her. "You're good at these sketches."

"Thank you."

He turned another page for a close-up of an employee at the carding machine. "This looks good. I'd like people in it. After all, they're our consumers."

She made a note. "Fine. Whatever you want, because this is just a rough draft. I'll lay it out and see what changes I think it needs. I'll have to get all the costs together, too."

Tath nodded. "If we get tied up by rainy weather, or are delayed for any other reason, will it cost more for filming?"

She shook her head. "No. We'll agree on the cost ahead

of time and it'll be a package deal. If we run into snags because of weather or whatever, it's our problem, not yours."

"I see. What time tomorrow do you leave for Dallas?"

"I'm driving, and I plan to leave early. I'll have to get Snuffy after I check out of the hotel. While you look at those sketches, Tath, I'll finish getting ready."

She rose and started to move away, but he reached up and took her arm to pull her down on his knees. "This is more interesting."

She smiled and twined her arms around his neck while he held her tightly and kissed her. She knew every kiss bound her more firmly to him—and opened her to more pain later. But she had no will to resist him. Despite the pain she knew she would feel, she couldn't resist the joy within her reach now. She looked at him through heavy lids and murmured, "Here goes sight-seeing..."

He kissed her ear and whispered, "I'll make you forget all about that..."

"Forget about what?" she asked and he chuckled. He raised his head and looked into her eyes.

"You're always so damn composed, Hilary."

She closed her eyes and raised her head while his lips trailed below her ear to her shoulder. "Look who's talking."

"You have to have the last word, too."

"Not necessarily," she replied. She felt his hands at her neck. The long zipper at the back of her dress made a faint scratching noise as he tugged it below her waist and pushed the garment off her shoulders.

She heard his sharp intake of breath as his head moved lower and he rained strategic kisses on her flesh until she moaned with pleasure. She was barely aware of Tath rising and lifting her effortlessly in his arms to move to the bed.

He switched off the bright overhead light, leaving only a small lamp burning on top of the dresser. In its dim glow, her skin was satiny and golden. Tath lowered her to the bed, then peeled away his clothes and flung them aside before he knelt to extricate her from the green dress and undo her undergarments.

When at last they were both naked, he stretched out and

gathered her into his arms. He kissed her passionately, with all the ardor he had shown in the demanding, possessive kiss earlier that day in his office.

She was lost to him. Looking at him mutely, she heard him say, "Tell me you'll miss me when you go back to Dallas, Hilary."

She squeezed her eyes shut. She couldn't let him see how vulnerable she was, how open and exquisitely sensitive she felt. During the day it wasn't difficult to act nonchalant and self-assured, but at night, in a moment of intimacy, she couldn't hide her true feelings.

She said quietly, "That works two ways. Will *you* miss *me*, Tath?"

"Of course I will." He said it simply, yet the words carried so much conviction that it was impossible to worry about all those women who hovered around him.

She gazed into his slate-gray eyes and couldn't breathe. His eyes darkened, confirming the depth of his feelings. Hilary tightened her arms around his neck and pulled him down to her. She wanted his mouth, his body, his heart. She shifted and murmured against his ear, "I only need you."

An exquisite torment befuddled her senses and diminished reality. Tath's hands moved over her, giving her a pleasure that was pure bliss.

She touched his hard, furred chest, his coppery, smooth skin, his long, muscular legs.

He paused to look at her. "This is what I feel, Hilary." He tilted her chin up. His fingers moved to her mouth to part her lips as he leaned forward to kiss her. His kiss was deep, demanding a wild response.

He shifted and moved between her thighs while his gaze traveled over her hungrily and his breathing became ragged. "You're so lovely . . ." he whispered hoarsely. She reached for him and he leaned down to explore her long legs, caressing her, sending streams of fire raging through her.

Through layers of drugged passion, she heard the ring of the phone. With an effort, she turned her head and looked at it, only a few feet away, on a table beside the bed. She gasped as Tath's lips trailed across her body. Another ring jarred the stillness.

"Tath," she whispered, winding her fingers in his luxurious curls, feeling the silky hairs with her hands. "My brother was supposed..." It was impossible to talk. It took too much effort when all her awareness, all her consciousness was on Tath and what he was doing to her.

Laying his cheek against her smooth, warm skin, he looked at her. His voice was a ragged whisper, "Go on, Hilary, answer it." He turned and his mouth touched her again, his tongue trailing along her hip while she twisted and locked her fingers tighter in his hair.

Above the roaring in her ears she heard another ring. It meant nothing. Her only thought was of Tath. "I'm not holding you back..." he whispered.

Belying his words, his hands and mouth held her as firmly as iron chains. She never knew when the phone stopped ringing; her attention was focused on the lean, passionate man holding her. She shifted to return his caresses, to evoke the same pounding heartbeat from him, the same hungry ecstasy that made them both want more and more.

He drove her to such need, such hunger, that she was wild with longing. And she knew he felt the same—he was as lost in her as she was in him. Her hands rested lightly on his narrow hips as she memorized him with her fingertips.

He groaned and moved to possess her, to drive her to impossible heights of passion and need and finally satisfaction.

Desire uncoiled and relented as Tath stretched out beside her. He pulled her against him, kissed her cheeks, temple, and ear, and murmured, "I love you, Hilary."

If only he meant it! Her heart soared, yet an inner voice warned her not to take the sweet words as a commitment.

Her eyelids felt heavy, her skin was damp and her hair in disarray. She wrapped her arm around his shoulder and kissed his throat while she whispered, "I'm glad the hotel didn't catch on fire. I couldn't have made it out."

He chuckled deep in his throat and shifted a bit to look

at her. His fingertips traced a line from her forehead to her shoulder. "I couldn't make it outside now," he replied. "You've demolished me."

"Where?" she asked in mocking tones. "Here?" She ran her fingertips over his sharp hipbone. "Or here?"

He laughed and caught her hand in his. "Cool it, lady, before you do me in completely."

"That's exactly what I want to do."

He rolled on his side and propped his head on his hand to gaze down at her. His other hand circled her waist to pull her tightly against him. He smiled into her eyes.

Hilary's heart turned over as she gazed up at him. She knew she was hopelessly in love. Blake Crowley faded to nothing. Tath was all and forever. She studied the creases bracketing his mouth when he smiled, the tiny bristles on his chin, the fine lines around the corners of his wide gray eyes. Every inch of him was precious to her, all-important. That he wouldn't return her love was a consideration she didn't want to face at the moment and she firmly closed her mind to it as she lay in Tath's arms.

"What are you thinking, Hilary?"

She looked at him. "How much I love you," she answered truthfully. She couldn't detect any change of expression in his face. He leaned forward and kissed her forehead, lightly and briefly, and settled beside her to hug her to him.

"How long before you'll be back in New Orleans?"

She thought about the commercials, the work that would be necessary to get everything ready to present to Tath.

"I should have the commercials prepared by the end of next week. I can come back Thursday."

She was aware of the change in conversation—of the intrusion of the outside world. There was no repetition of Tath's declaration of love, and she knew he had spoken in a mere moment of passion. She tried to ignore a twinge of pain.

"I'm cheating you."

She looked up at him. "What are you talking about?"

"I promised you dinner and sight-seeing."

With exaggeration, she said, "I'm seeing some pretty

impressive sights right now." She ran her fingers across his bare chest, and he laughed.

He shifted to look down at her. "I promised to feed you, and I keep my promises. Come on." He rose, and Hilary gazed at his strong, vigorous body. She turned away sharply and pulled on her clothes as quickly as possible.

As she struggled with the zipper of her dress, she felt his fingers take hold and pull it closed. He remarked dryly, "You must be hungry as hell. That's the fastest dressing I've seen in a long time."

She turned to look at him. "If I don't hurry, we might not get out of here tonight."

His eyes darkened and he drew a sharp breath. He reached out to slip his arm around her waist.

Hilary stepped into his arms and raised her mouth for his kiss. Emotions filled her—amazement that his kiss was as powerful, as tantalizing as before. She felt regret that it was so devastating to her, and she experienced a sweeping need that drove all other feelings out of existence.

After a moment he released her. "You're right. Come on, or we won't get out of here."

He took her hand and headed for the door. She laughed and shook free. "Not that fast, Tath! Let me brush my hair. I know it's a tangle."

She moved to the dresser and picked up her hairbrush to pull it through the burnished curls. She glanced over her shoulder in the mirror and saw Tath leaning against the door, a cigarette in his mouth, watching her.

"Stop that," she said.

He raised both hands and smiled, the cigarette dangling from the corner of his mouth. Again he reminded her of a buccaneer. "I'm not doing anything."

She put down the brush and turned to pick up her purse. "Oh, no, not much! Those looks are like a blast from a blowtorch."

He laughed and took her arm to step into the hall. "You provoke them."

Tath took her down to the car and drove to the French Quarter. Between Jackson Square and the river, he parked and took her hand. "Let's walk around a little. There's a superb restaurant here."

Tath took her to the Andrew Jackson. Through a recessed doorway in the peach-colored stucco building, they entered a dark, narrow interior. Hilary gazed at the huge mural of Andrew Jackson before they followed the maître d' past tables with starched white tablecloths and lovely silver. As soon as they sat down in an alcove, the headwaiter appeared.

After a delicious dinner of trout Ponchartrain and soft-shelled crab, they strolled in the direction of the riverfront. Hand in hand, they walked along the levee until they stopped at an outdoor shop to purchase café au lait and beignets, the square, holeless French doughnuts that were a New Orleans specialty.

They sat and listened to the muffled sounds from the docks, watching the barges and cargo ships, the lights on the glistening river, while a soft breeze blew across them.

After a time, Tath said, "I'm not the marrying kind, Hilary."

She laughed. "I think this is an old conversation. I told you in your office—there are no strings attached. So stop with the explanations. Tath. There's no need for them."

He studied her. "I hope you mean that."

She sobered and looked at him. Heaven help her. Solemnly she said, "I do."

In a subdued mood they drove back to Tath's boat. Hilary spent a glorious evening in his arms on the deck beneath a bright, star-filled sky. Yet throughout their fevered love-making and murmured endearments she kept hearing his cutting words: *I'm not the marrying kind.*

Early the next morning, Tath took her to the hotel and kissed her good-bye. Along with Snuffy, she left for Dallas.

When she consulted with her brothers, both were pleased with the progress she had made on the Justin commercials. Hilary developed the storyboard, calculated the proposed budget, and gathered information to present to Tath. To her surprise he called every night, and it seemed an eternity to her until the week was over and she boarded a plane for New Orleans.

- 13 -

IT WAS THURSDAY afternoon when she turned her rental car into the parking lot of the mill. As she crossed the lot, her pulse beat faster. Holding a red purse that matched the trim on her white blouse and skirt, she carried in her other hand a briefcase with the storyboard and proposal for the commercials.

After greeting Kitty, she waited while the secretary pressed an intercom button and announced, "Miss O'Brien from Visual Communications is here."

Tath's voice came clearly through the speaker. "Send her in."

It was like a blow to her midsection to face him again. Dressed in a pastel green shirt, a pale gray tie, and charcoal slacks, he came around the desk. As he crossed the room to her, his eyes devoured her with a look that accelerated her already pounding heart.

Without hesitation, he took her in his arms and leaned down to kiss her. His kiss was everything she'd remembered, and more. She stood on tiptoe and returned it, relishing the feel of his shoulders beneath her fingers and his long, hard body bent over hers.

It was impossible to get close enough to him. Finally he released her, saying, "I'm ready to quit work for today."

She smiled. "Not so fast. I have a commercial to discuss with you."

"I'd like to see the day I come first in your life," he said mockingly, but there was a solemn look in his eyes that contradicted his tone of voice.

"Maybe that'll be the day *I* come first in *your* life, Tath."

His arms slipped around her and he leaned down to kiss her again. It was a wild, hungry kiss that took away her breath. When he finally released her, he said, "Now, what was that about a commercial?"

"I don't know," she whispered, and pulled him to her to kiss him again. His passionate response stirred an all-consuming longing within her.

Finally he looked down at her. "That's more like it. Let's look at your information and then let's go."

He released her and Hilary gazed down at herself in dismay. "Tath . . . my clothes. They look as if I pulled them out of the laundry hamper."

He grinned. "The moral to that, Hilary, is to take them off first."

"Or to keep you at arm's length!"

He chuckled and pulled a chair beside his. "Sit down here. How's our friend Snuffy?"

"As I told you on the phone, I decided not to bring him this time. A girlfriend of mine is boarding him, and I'm afraid she's spoiling him rotten."

Tath chuckled again. "Aw, don't be so hard on the little guy, Hilary. After all, he did bring us together originally, you know."

She groaned. "Among other things he did. Anyway, he's in good hands with Beth. And now, to business," she added briskly, seating herself and spreading a folder in front of him. She placed the storyboard next to the folder and watched as Tath began to turn the pages, carefully scrutinizing each sketch.

She scooted closer and turned back to the first sketch of the storyboard. "I thought we'd start with a scene taken from a helicopter and a five-second close shot of cotton plants beneath the oaks."

Tath turned to the next panel and Hilary continued, "We'll pan, moving above the fields of cotton. This would last ten seconds."

When he turned to another panel, she said, "Here's another long shot, zooming in above the mill for five seconds . . ." She reached out to turn the page. "Another five seconds with a picture of bales of cotton unloaded at the mill."

She looked at him. "That would be the first twenty-five seconds of film—all outside shots, one close and the others long shots or pans."

He looked at her. "Sounds fine so far." He turned the page and Hilary said, "The next fifteen seconds would be moving through the mill, showing the machinery and people at work . . ." She reached over to show him the next sketch. "Now a five-second close-up of a worker in dyeing or print-making—whatever you prefer, but some colorful part of the process . . ."

"I'd prefer printmaking."

"Okay. Next, a five-second close shot of bolts of fabric." She turned to another panel. "For the last ten seconds, various shots, close-up and long, of models wearing clothes made from Justin cotton."

Tath turned the panels and studied her sketches. She waited quietly until he raised his head. "I don't want the models at the end of the commercial. That's not part of my business."

She glanced down at her sketch. "I put that in because it ties everything up for the consumer. Here's your product in its final use. It shows the reason for what you do."

He frowned. "I don't know. This is bound to run up the cost." Before she could speak, he added quickly, "It isn't *just* the cost, Hilary. I know what you mean, but it doesn't have anything to do with my mills."

"But that's your material on the models. Your objective is to make the consumer want to wear Justin cotton."

"Sure, that's what I want ultimately, but the mills don't design dresses. That isn't my business. I don't want the final shot of the models."

Hilary tilted her head and asked softly, "It isn't because you don't trust a woman's judgment, is it?"

He flushed. "I wouldn't be working with you if I didn't trust your judgment." She recognized the stubborn thrust of his jaw. "I don't think your question is pertinent."

She wondered if she had guessed correctly. She didn't

want to point out that she had made more commercials than he had or that she knew promotion better than he did. She suspected he wasn't viewing her proposal with the objectivity he would have felt toward the work of a mere business associate—a male business associate.

"Well, then think about it, Tath, as you study my proposal. After all, it's your commercial, but give it some thought before you ax the idea."

"Sure. What will the commercial cost?"

She moved the storyboard to one side and opened the folder in front of him to go over the itemized costs.

"We do this with free-lance talent, Tath, and rental equipment. I've done the script and Hank will write the music. Jake is line producer, and he'll take care of props and getting everything together. I have an excellent cameraman lined up. Here are the estimated breakdowns."

He gazed at the figures and made some notations on a pad. "What are 'grips'?"

"They carry props, and otherwise help with the set."

"And gaffers?"

"The electricians. We have an audio studio with musical equipment and a control room where we'll do the music."

"What about the thirty-second spots?"

"The cost is figured in for all three commercials. You said it would be fine to take the two thirty-second commercials from shots in the sixty-second one."

"That's right."

"I've put them together, but any changes you want we can do easily."

She pulled the storyboard in front of him again and sat quietly while he looked at the scenes she had selected for the short commercials. His eyelashes were thick and dark above his prominent cheekbones as he examined her pictures.

He raised his head and asked, "How long will it take to shoot all this?"

"We can do it in a day, in good weather. Here's the slogan—'Count on Justin cotton'—and here's the script to go with those shots." She shifted the papers spread before him and continued, "As you can see, there will be very little dialogue. The commercial will rely on music, background singing of the name Justin Cotton and the slogan, 'Count on Justin cotton.' After we shoot the scenes, we'll put the music with it and present it to you for your approval or suggestions."

Tath moved back to the budget, gazed at the figures, and ran his finger down the column. While he read, Hilary sat quietly until he finally closed the folder and looked at her. "I'll study this and let you know tomorrow."

"Fine."

He turned to place his hand against her cheek. "Now let's get out of here and worry about business later."

"Can you do that?" She wondered what decision he'd made about his mother's offer to take the job at the mill permanently, but she didn't want to ask.

"I certainly can." He stood and gathered up her material as well as a folder of his own, which he placed in his briefcase. He took her arm.

Hilary smoothed her wrinkled skirt again. "Tath, I'm embarrassed to walk out of here. I'll know better next time."

"Next time wear Justin cotton." He flashed her a rakish smile. When they emerged from the mill into the hot sunshine, Hilary said, "I need to check into a hotel."

"Why don't you just phone the St. Jean from my boat and make a reservation?" Tath suggested. "I don't think I can wait much longer to be alone with you."

She smiled. "So you're into instant gratification are you?"

He gave her a look of mock petulance as they approached her car. "You mean you're not just as eager to be with me, Hilary?"

"I think you know the answer to that question," she said softly, looking up at his handsome face as he leaned against the car door and held her chin in the palm of his hand. "Now don't give me that wounded look," she teased. "After all, we do have all evening to be together."

"True, but I still owe you some sightseeing, and we'll also have to put in an appearance at Mother's birthday party."

"Oh, Tath," she blurted out before she could check her

disappointment. She was certain that Mrs. Justin would be no more delighted to see her tonight than she had been at the last party. And Hilary had been looking forward to a romantic evening alone with Tath.

He put both hands on her shoulders and gave them a tender squeeze. "I'm sorry the party is tonight, Hilary, but I can't skip it. We won't have to stay very long."

"I understand, but, Tath, maybe you should just go by yourself and pick me up at the hotel afterward."

"No," he said firmly. "It's bad enough we have to go out to the boat in separate cars—I'm not spending even fifteen minutes apart from you after that."

"But—"

"No buts, Hilary. Now why are we standing out here talking when we could be on my boat . . ." His voice trailed off suggestively. "I'll start up the Porsche and you follow me. And be prepared to break a few speed records," he added with a mischievous gleam in his eyes.

His tone brooked no argument, and Hilary smiled her acquiescence as he opened the car door for her and then loped off to the Porsche.

Tath had only been half jesting about breaking speed records, she discovered as she found herself having to press the accelerator almost to the floorboard to keep up with him on the highway. She thought they deserved a place in the *Guinness Book of Records* for getting from the mill to the dock in such a short time.

Tath came over to her car as she was lifting her suitcase from the trunk. "I'd like to change out of my traveling clothes," she explained as he deftly picked up the suitcase with one hand and snaked his other arm around her waist.

An exaggerated leer came over his face. "You'll be out of your traveling clothes before you know it," he teased in a low voice. "If it weren't for this damned suitcase," he continued, "I'd scoop you into my arms and spirit you off to my lair as quick as summer lightning, my lovely."

His swashbuckling tone, and the fact that they were crossing the plank to the boat, suddenly brought back to Hilary the image of Tath as a pirate, and she laughed.

"This is no laughing matter, my beauty," he went on in the same melodramatic vein as he guided her onto the aft deck. "Prepare to be ravished, my lady love!"

"Prepare *yourself*, Sir Francis Drake," she joked back. "Welcome to the twentieth century, where a woman can do some ravishing herself."

"Ahha!" he said, setting down her suitcase and twirling an imaginary mustache. "I'm all for affirmative action, my little minx, with the emphasis on *action*." And with that, he drew her into his arms and covered her neck with searing kisses, sending pinpricks of need to her very core. Wordlessly he lifted her in his arms and strode toward the large master stateroom. With an adept kick, he opened the door and deposited her gently on the large bed, as if she were some precious cargo. "Lord, Hilary, how I want you," he said as he stretched out beside her and captured her in a fierce embrace.

"I want you, too, Tath," she answered softly, relaxing in the dim, peaceful atmosphere of the room. Narrow, shuttered oval windows shut out the sun's bright rays. But she soon lost all consciousness of their surroundings as Tath's lips crashed down on hers and his tongue probed her mouth with sweet urgency.

He was all she remembered, and more. Her heart pounded with hammerblows that roared in her ears and drowned out all other sounds. Tath unzipped her skirt and dropped it off the bed. His fingers shook slightly as he undid the buttons of her blouse, then discarded it atop the skirt. He drew a sharp breath as he looked at her. "You'll never know how much I missed you, Hilary."

Before she could answer, he leaned forward to kiss her while his hands removed the rest of her clothing to bare her flesh to his eyes, his mouth, and his hands.

Next his own clothes dropped away and Hilary's hands explored and caressed his fine-textured, smooth skin. In the soft light of the room, his body was bronze. Dark shadows played over his rippling muscles as he twisted and shifted to touch her.

She caught his face between her hands and paused to

look up at him. "Oh, Tath, Tath," she whispered, tugging his head gently toward hers for a kiss.

Her hands slid along his spine, following its curve across the middle of his back. He looked at her through half-closed eyes. His breathing was quick as he leaned back, kneeling beside her while his gaze traveled where his hands had been.

He reached out and his warm fingertips caressed her flesh, causing her to gasp with pleasure. He eased himself on top of her, slipping his arms beneath her to hold her close.

"I love you, Hilary," he whispered. "While you were gone, being with you was all I thought about, all I remembered."

"I know. I feel the same, Tath."

He became still and asked, "Did you feel that way when you were in Dallas?"

"You know I did. I told you that each night on the phone." She ran her hand across his chest, the short hairs tickling her palm. His eyes blazed with desire. His hands moved along her side, sending heat coursing through her, heightening her smoldering need for him.

She knew she needed him badly. She felt incomplete without him, as if some vital part of her were missing. She leaned forward to kiss his hard shoulder. Her lips moved to his throat, to his ear. He groaned and twisted to pull her into his arms. His kiss possessed her utterly, demanding her passionate response, until he moved and his lips trailed over her body, touching her soft flesh to drive her to breathless longing.

He whispered in her ear, "Without you, I feel incomplete."

Dimly she heard his words expressing what she felt for him, but she was beyond answering. Her head thrashed back and forth as his hands stroked her sensitve skin.

Desire uncoiled, spread, and became unbearable. She moaned and slid her hands along his lean, muscular arms.

He shifted and moved above her. Lovingly he entered her and she welcomed the completion they had both yearned for. As Tath joined her and filled her and moved her in an ageless rhythm of love, Hilary clung to him, yielding herself totally to merge with him in ever more frenzied movements until he drove her to a shuddering fulfillment and met her there.

Finally he sank down beside her and pulled her to him to embrace her. He smoothed her red-hued curls away from her face and lifted the heavy tresses of hair off her neck.

He leaned forward and kissed her lightly. "You're beautiful and I feel impossibly lucky."

His arms tightened to pull her close, and she could hear the wild pounding of his heart. As she lay still in his arms, his pulse gradually returned to a normal rate. "It was difficult to keep from doing this in my office today," he said.

She smiled. "Thank goodness I got you out of there in time."

"Hilary, I'd like to meet your family. I've met Hank, but I haven't met Jake or your father."

She looked up in surprise. His chin was close. She ran her finger over his jaw and across his firm lips. "I'll be glad for you to meet them. You'll have to come to Dallas to meet my father. When we film, Jake will be here."

He trailed his fingers across her shoulder. "How can you shoot all that commercial in one day?"

"Are you thinking about business at a time like this?" she reproached him playfully. "Or is this your revenge for the damage you accused me of doing to your ego before?"

He turned on his side and propped his head up on his hand to look at her. "I couldn't put a dent in that cool exterior of yours."

"My, you make me sound like the original Snow Queen."

He shook his head. "Not in the least. You're just very collected and self-assured."

How little he knows, she thought. She was hopelessly, absolutely in love with him. She hadn't known what love really was until she met Tath. She thought of all the things she liked about him: his warm sense of humor and quick laugh, his teasing and good nature, his self-assurance and commanding personality.

"What are you thinking?"

She studied him. "How much I love you."

He looked at her solemnly for a minute, then he said, "I only hope it's as much as I love you." In a lighter tone, but with a look of adoration in his eyes, he asked, "Shall we count the ways?"

She smiled. "That would take a day and a night—at least."

Abruptly she sat up. "That reminds me—I'd better call the Hotel St. Jean and reserve a room for tonight."

He frowned and pulled her beside him again, nuzzling her neck gently. "Forget the hotel, Hilary. Don't you want to spend the night here, with me?"

"Of course I do," she said tenderly. "But, Tath, what if Hank calls the hotel and tries to leave a message for me? As far as my brothers know, you and I are business associates, period."

"I see," he said quietly, then countered quickly, "What if you told them we're engaged?"

"You want me to lie to them, Tath?" she asked incredulously.

He shook his head, a look of frustration coming over his features. "Oh, Hilary. I'd planned to wait for an appropriate time and place, but, hell, I can't hold back my feelings another minute. I've never felt about any woman the way I feel about you. I didn't realize how much I need you until you went back to Dallas and I couldn't see you, touch you, be with you. I want to spend the rest of my life with you, darling. Every moment of it."

A joyful radiance pervaded her, yet she hardly dared believe her ears. Could he mean—oh, no, not Tath Justin. He'd made his position crystal clear. Still—

His next words removed all her doubts. "What I want you to tell your brothers isn't a lie, Hilary. I'm asking you to marry me. I want that more than anything in the world."

- 14 -

AFTER THE FIRST stunned moment, she let out her breath and sat up. "Oh, Tath..." she breathed, and then she was in his arms, crushed to him while he kissed her as hungrily as he had in the office when she'd first arrived.

Finally he released her slightly and smiled at her. His eyes danced with excitement and she felt as if she would burst with happiness. "Tath, I can't believe..."

Her words faded again as another passionate kiss answered her, more definitively than any words could. This time when he released her, Hilary looked at him silently, holding back speech while she tried to think about what had happened.

Never had she expected him to propose to her. Never. It was impossible, unbelievable! At that moment she thought of Blake Crowley, of her first engagement and Blake's proposal. She hadn't been ecstatic, as she was now, but the moment she thought of Blake, she thought of Mrs. Justin.

History repeats itself, she thought. How could she fall in love with a man whose background was the same as Blake's? She recalled how Mrs. Justin couldn't even remember her name. She tilted her head to one side and asked Tath, "Does your mother know you've asked me?"

His dark brows came together over the bridge of his nose. "What the hell does that have to do with anything. No, Hilary, she doesn't. No one knows except you and me."

She drew in a sharp breath. She'd made him angry, but it was impossible to forget Mrs. Justin's attitude. "She might not approve."

He swore softly. "She'll approve, don't worry."

With his words, a new thought struck Hilary. She sat up and looked at him. "Are you staying with the mill? Did you tear up that check your mother made out to your exploration group?"

"I haven't decided."

She felt a cold, hard knot begin to form inside her. His words rang in her ears. "You haven't decided?" she echoed. "The most important thing in your life, and you haven't come to a conclusion?" Suddenly she knew why he had proposed to her.

He had succumbed to family pressure. He'd stay with the mill, get married, and settle down. And live with his mother and Elliot Compton running his affairs forever. In time perhaps he'd regret his decision and the loss of his freedom, and resent his wife for chaining him to a dull routine. "Your mother won't approve," she whispered. "I know she won't."

"Yes, she will, and to hell with it if she doesn't."

"You don't mean that. You've asked me to marry you to please them."

"I asked you to please myself—and I thought you'd be pleased, too," he retorted sharply, running a hand through his dark curls. "Besides, you're contradicting yourself, Hilary. You accuse me of marrying to please my mother, but at the same time you insist that she won't be pleased."

"Perhaps that's the idea," she speculated aloud, trying to sort out her confused thoughts. "You don't dare defy your mother outright by refusing to take over the mill, but you'll defy her to the extent of marrying someone she considers unsuitable." She wondered suddenly if Blake's proposal, too, hadn't been an attempt to get out from under his mother's thumb—only he hadn't had the courage to go through with it.

"Hilary, that's absurd!" Tath stormed. "And I'm insulted that you'd suspect me of using you as a pawn in some struggle that you imagine is going on between Mother and me."

"I imagine it?" she challenged. "Why, the tension between you is so thick you could cut it with a knife. You told me yourself that she's trying to manipulate you."

"And I'm not letting myself be manipulated. I didn't ask Mary Lynn Weber to marry me, did I?"

"That's not the point. You may not even be conscious of what you're doing, Tath. But I can see how you might salvage your pride by marrying me against your mother's wishes to compensate for giving in to the rest of her plans for you, instead of following your own heart—"

"You couldn't be more wrong!" he exploded. "Can't you understand—my heart isn't where it was last week. You've caused a revolution in it. I still love oceanography, but the idea of roving over the seven seas with a girl in every port has lost its charm for me. I want you, Hilary. I want to come home to you every night. I want to have children with you."

The knot in her heart seemed to dissolve and melt, like an ice cube in warm water, but as he spoke Hilary realized how little she knew this man. How could she believe that all his desires and plans had been so radically transformed in a mere week?

"I don't know what to say, Tath," she admitted honestly. "Everything's happened so quickly, and you've done such a hundred-and-eighty-degree turnaround. Last week you said you weren't the marrying kind. You didn't want to be tied down . . ."

"Haven't you ever changed your mind?"

She saw the fire in his eyes, but she had to know the truth. "Of course, but not about something so basic and important. What about the mill? You've told me repeatedly that it gets to you, that you want to be an oceanographer. Now suddenly you're capitulating, letting yourself be black-mailed with those checks—"

"The checks have nothing to do with it!" he shouted. "It's my love for you that's caused me to reconsider, Hilary."

Was he only appealing to her vanity? Perhaps he didn't really love her at all. The thought made her feel utterly desolate, hollow.

"Look," he continued, "I haven't capitulated. I told you,

I just haven't made up my mind about the mill yet. In the end I may not accept Mother's and Elliot's offer, but it's not a decision to be made lightly. Because of you, the idea of settling down is a damned sight more attractive to me now than it was last week. Perhaps even then I exaggerated my gripes about the mill to you. I didn't want it forced on me, but if I choose it for my own reasons, that's an entirely different matter. If I really hated the business, I wouldn't have gotten involved in it at all, Hilary, not even temporarily. I'm not the milksop you seem to think I am."

"Tath, I never said—"

"You didn't have to," he interrupted bitterly, again running his hand through his tousled curls. "A little while ago you said you loved me—"

"I do love you, Tath."

"Then say you'll marry me. No ifs, ands, or buts. Just say yes, Hilary."

She gave a groan of exasperation. "Tath, first things first. You have to decide about your professional future before we talk about marriage."

"Do I have to have a specific occupation to get you to marry me?" he demanded, his eyes shooting sparks. "I would think if you really loved me, what I do for a living wouldn't matter."

"It matters that you run your own life, that you know what you want—"

"I want you, Hilary! How many times do I have to say it? But it doesn't look as if you want me. Maybe you meant what you said at first about not being in any hurry to settle down. Does the idea of commitment frighten you? Is that why you broke off your engagement to Blake Crowley?"

"I didn't break off my engagement to Blake. It was Mrs. Crow—" She checked herself, but it was too late.

"Mrs. Crowley," he said, eyeing her intently. "There was a Mrs. Crowley—a disapproving Mrs. Crowley? And there's a disapproving Mrs. Justin, too, isn't there? I begin to understand why you keep harping on my mother, Hilary. Hell, I know she's been none too gracious so far, but believe me, she'll come around. She was angry because she thought I preferred a frivolous flirtation with you to a proper courtship of one of her marriage-minded debutantes. But when she realizes that because of you I *want* to settle down, she'll relent—she'll even be grateful to you. I know my mother, Hilary. Please trust me."

A wild hope surged in her heart, but as quickly ebbed. Tath might be capable of an instant transformation, but she could hardly believe the same of the frosty Mrs. Justin. Besides, there was still the issue of his future. "I just can't talk about it any more, Tath," she said. "You still have to make your decision—"

"No, Hilary, *you* have to make *your* decision. For better or for worse, for richer or for poorer, in sickness and in health—yes or no?"

"I won't be stonewalled, Tath," she snapped. "We both need time to think. I'm going to make a reservation at the St. Jean now, and then I'm getting dressed and going to the hotel to mull things over. I don't think I can face your mother's birthday celebration tonight. Why don't you do some reflecting, too, and then call me after you leave the party."

"Hilary, you can't walk out on me like this. We're spending the evening together, party and all."

"No! Stop bullying me, Tath. I'm going to the hotel— and I'm staying there for the evening." With trembling fingers she reached for the bedside telephone and dialed information to ask the number of the hotel. Tath watched in grim silence as she made her calls.

"All right, then," he said gruffly. "You've obviously made your choice. "I'll get dressed, too, and drive you to the St. Jean."

"That won't be necessary. It would only be awkward for both of us," she said, turning her back to him as she got up and began to put on her undergarments. Her nakedness made her feel vulnerable, and she was anxious to get dressed and leave. But when she picked up her wrinkled blouse, she could only look at it in dismay.

"You wanted to change into a fresh outfit," Tath's voice came from the bed. "I'll get my things on and fetch your suitcase from the deck."

"Thank you." Still feeling an instinct to cover herself, she backed toward the bed and slipped under the covers as Tath rose and began to pick up his clothing from the floor. At the sight of his smooth, bronzed skin, taut muscles, and narrow waist, Hilary felt a pang of longing. Resisting the impulse to pull him back to her, to press herself against his lean, powerful physique and feel his arms close around her in a materful embrace, she warned herself not to be swayed by mere passion. Yet she knew that her feelings for Tath were much more than mere sexual desire. She loved him, she wanted to marry him, but why couldn't he see how important it was that he decide about his own future first?

Tath dressed hurriedly and left her without a word, to fetch the suitcase. When he returned and deposited the valise by the side of the bed, Hilary nodded her thanks and quickly bent over the suitcase, grateful for the excuse to keep her tear-filled eyes lowered. She took out a deep blue sundress and hastily stepped into it.

"Here, let me." She felt Tath's warm fingers at the zipper of the dress, and willed herself not to tremble at his touch. As she slipped her feet into her sandals, she felt his hands at her waist, gently revolving her to face him.

"You're so lovely, Hilary," he said as he looked into her eyes. Her vision was blurred by the tears that threatened to spill onto her cheeks, and her throat was too choked for her to say a word. For long moments they simply stared at each other in pain and yearning.

Finally she forced herself to speak. "I'd better leave now, Tath."

"At least let me drive you back."

"No. Tath, please. I need to be alone." She broke from his grasp and saw his jaw tighten as she wrenched free.

"Have it your own way, then. But we have a date tonight, Hilary."

"That's canceled. Oh, Tath, we'd only start arguing again. Go to your mother's party. We'll be working together on the commercials, so we'll still see each other. After you come to a conclusion about your future, we'll talk."

"We have a date tonight, Hilary," he repeated.

She shook her head. He spoke quietly, but she noticed that his fingers were balled into tight fists, his knuckles pale where the skin pulled taut. Her heart felt as if it were squeezed inside his fist. She wanted to say yes, to promise him all her love forever.

As they looked wordlessly at each other, she felt her insides twist ever tighter. It took a heart-wrenching effort to turn away and start for the stateroom door.

"You're forgetting your suitcase," he said, picking up the valise and striding alongside her to the aft deck.

Misery made a heavy weight in her heart as she left the boat with him and they walked to her car. As she fumbled in her pocketbook for her keys, she said, "Good-bye, Tath. I'll see you in the morning about the commercials. What time will be best for you?"

He compressed his lips for a moment before answering stiffly, "How about ten o'clock?"

"Fine. I'll come to your office." Quickly she opened the trunk of the car and Tath hefted her suitcase inside. Clutching her keys, she opened the car door and got into the driver's seat.

As she turned on the ignition, she could see him out of the corner of her eye, standing a few feet from the car with his hands on his hips. The motor jumped to life and she roared off before she could change her mind, turn back, and throw herself into his arms.

- 15 -

ON THE WAY to the hotel, Hilary brooded over the angry exchange that had occurred between Tath and herself on the boat. Was she sacrificing her life's happiness to foolish prudence, she wondered as she gazed out at the golden western sky. Being with Tath felt so right. She cherished the affectionate banter they enjoyed, the professional respect they had for each other, the physical intimacy that brought her ecstasy and a sense of utter wholeness. She was sure she would never love another man as she loved Tath, yet a voice of inner logic cautioned that she had known him only a short time, and already practical problems created dark clouds on the horizon of their future together.

No—Tath had to come to grips with his own career choice before they could begin to contemplate a permanent commitment to each other. She didn't dare speculate about their life together until he had come to a decision—one that was his own, not his mother's.

So ran her thoughts, but her heart wasn't in them. Her innermost being was lost to Tath, ached for him with an intensity that was beyond any emotion she had ever known before.

By the time she checked into the Hotel St. Jean and turned the key of her room, Hilary felt emotionally drained, exhausted. The luxurious appointments of her accommodations seemed sterile and empty, and she was conscious only of how lonely and tired she felt. She experienced a fleeting regret that she hadn't brought along Snuffy, who at least would have greeted her eagerly after this traumatic afternoon, until she remembered that the hotel didn't allow animals in any case. With a long sigh she flung herself on the bed. Her despondency was too deep even for tears, and she yielded to the numbness that spread rapidly through her limbs. Soon she was asleep.

She was awakened by an insistent knocking at her door. She opened her eyes to total darkness, hastily switched on the bedside lamp, and rifled through her suitcase for her traveling alarm clock. It was nine o'clock.

"Who is it?" she called dazedly as she rose and stumbled to the door.

She heard a muffled voice call out a name that sounded like "Frank." She didn't know any Frank; she wondered hazily if it was her brother Hank. But why would Hank be in New Orleans? And it didn't sound like his voice.

She unlocked the door and opened it a crack. She stared through the narrow opening at a face that brought her instantly awake.

Tath! Her initial joy at seeing his ruggedly handsome features was replaced instantly by indignation.

"You said Frank!" she accused. "You barged up here under false pretenses."

"Sure, I said Frank. Short for Sir Francis. I seemed to have more success with you as an Elizabethan pirate than in my own person, so I thought I'd better announce myself as him," came the familiar rich baritone. A mahogany loafer wedged itself into the opening before she could close the door. "I want to talk to you, Hilary."

"What is there to say?" she asked helplessly, registering the perfect fit of his white denims and the casual draping of the blue sweater she had bought him across his broad shoulders, over a fawn-colored handkerchief-linen shirt.

"Hilary, let me in," he ordered gruffly.

Mechanically she opened the door and Tath entered. Taking in his impeccable appearance, she was conscious of how rumpled the dress she had slept in must appear.

"I took a nap," she explained, trying to smooth the sundress.

"Mmm, you look rested and luscious," he crooned, wrapping his arms around her and hugging her to him.

"I'll bet! Well, you certainly can't say the same for my dress, which you're wrinkling even more."

"When will you ever learn to wear Justin cotton?" he reproached her playfully as his fingers toyed with the wispy tendrils of hair at the nape of her neck.

"Tath, stop," she gasped. "What are you doing here? Your mother's party . . ."

"Is going great guns," he finished for her. "I stopped by on my way here to wish her many happy returns. We can drop in again later if you like, but it's not obligatory."

"Why did you come?" she demanded, wriggling to extricate herself from his viselike grip. The heady scent of him intoxicated her, and she felt a strange reluctance to tear herself away.

"To take you out," he replied breezily, pressing her even closer to his virile body. "Oh, Hilary, Hilary, you feel so good. Aren't you even the least bit glad to see me?"

"I don't know," she said warily, though all her nerves were responding to his caresses. "I told you our date was canceled."

"And I told you it wasn't. Lady mine, I don't take no for an answer." His actions affirmed his words as he nuzzled her neck with burning lips.

"Tath—"

"Hilary, Hilary. Did I ever tell you how much I like your name?" he said softly.

"Tath, you're tormenting me." Her insides were jelly, and her knees foam rubber.

"Good. *You* torment *me*, Hilary, twenty-four hours a day. In a minute I'll forget that I came here for a special purpose, so you'd better get changed and let's go."

"Go?" she echoed. "Where?"

"I want to surprise you," he murmured.

"I'll have to take a bath," she said faintly.

"I'd like to take one with you. But no, that would be fatal. Take a shower—a quick shower," he advised. "I'll have a cigarette while I wait for you."

"Mr. Marlboro Man," she teased, gliding from his embrace.

"Hilary's man," he corrected. "Woman, take a shower and get dressed. Nothing too fancy—I'll choose something from your suitcase while you're in the bathroom."

"But, Tath—"

"Hilary, I'm not asking, I'm telling you." As he'd done earlier on his houseboat, he grasped the end of an imaginary mustache and rolled it between his fingers. Again she saw him vividly as a pirate chief, and to her surprise she felt no desire to argue further.

"Aye, Aye, Captain," she replied, and started toward the bathroom.

She emerged some minutes later, wrapped in a fluffy, rose-colored towel.

"Mmm—sweet torture," Tath groaned as he gazed at her hungrily. "But never mind—I've laid out your clothes on the bed. Dress and let us be gone, my lovely."

Enchanted by his piratical manner, Hilary made no protest. She donned the black chinos and canary-colored chiffon shirt, modestly keeping her back to Tath as she did so.

"Can't you give me a clue as to where we're going, Tath?" she cajoled him as she dressed.

"I can, but I won't. I'm hoping you're a sucker for surprises," he said lightly.

"Just a little hint," she coaxed.

"Okay, a very little one," he said, cocking a dark eyebrow at her as she turned to face him while she buttoned her blouse. "It has something to do with my past—a secret past of which you know nothing."

"Sounds sinister," she said hesitantly, stepping into her sandals.

"Not sinister but delightful," he assured her. "A new aspect of your New Orleans experience."

"But you didn't really give me a hint," she said. "If it has something to do with a past I know nothing of, how can I guess?"

"You can't, and you won't be tempted to back out, because curiosity has gotten the better of you," he said smoothly. "Now stop being so logical and let's go enjoy ourselves."

The gleaming black Porsche awaited them a few blocks

from the hotel. As the engine roared to life and they shot out of the parking space, Hilary leaned against the glove-leather upholstery and wondered about their destination. Tath maneuvered the car deftly through the streets of New Orleans to the outskirts of town.

Beneath a starlit sky she eventually saw a blaze of neon lights ahead. "It looks like an amusement park," she said.

"Good guess," he replied, pulling into a large parking lot already crowded with cars. "It's actually a traveling carnival, but you had the right idea."

Gazing across the street at the twinkling lights of a Ferris wheel, Hilary asked, "But what has this to do with your past, Tath?"

He turned off the ignition and faced her across the seats of the Porsche. "Hilary," he said with mock solemnity, "I'm a former First-of-Mayer."

"A what?"

He chuckled. "That's carnival jargon for a short-timer. After my freshman year at Tulane, I had a summer job working for one of the visiting carnivals."

"But Mardi Gras is in February or March," she said, perplexed.

"True. But in the spring there are always touring carnivals pitched out here for a few months," he explained. "And I spent a summer working for one."

"Your mother..." she said without thinking.

"Considered it the height of vulgarity," he finished for her. "But she learned to live with my decision." He smiled winsomely. "You see, Hilary, from a young age I've been my own person."

As he opened the car door, Hilary heard the beguiling sounds of hurdy-gurdy music. She waited as Tath slid from the driver's seat and came around to open the passenger's door for her.

"You worked in a carnival?" she asked incredulously as his arm slipped around her waist and they strolled toward the bright lights and gay music. "What did you do?"

"Assisted one of the concessionaires who had no family

to help him out as most of them do," Tath explained. "He was having some kind of voice problem, so mainly I was a barker, a pitchman. You know, 'Step right up, ladies and gentlemen, fifty cents buys you three tosses of the baseball . . .'"

"I don't believe it!" Hilary laughed as they walked to the lot where the carnival was set up. "Your poor mother . . ."

"As I told you, she didn't approve, but I did it anyway. So you see, I'm not tied to Mama's apron strings."

"You brought me here to tell me that?"

"No, I brought you here to have a good time," he replied. "This isn't the outfit I worked for—they stopped coming years ago. I just thought we needed to get away from it all—and maybe I wanted to break down that cool exterior of yours and see you loosen up."

"I feel like a teenager again," she admitted. "When I was in high school in Dallas, occasionally we got a gang together to go to Six Flags Over Texas, and I always looked forward to those excursions."

"Six Flags Over Texas?" Tath inquired. "Is that the Disneyland of Dallas or what?"

"It's in Arlington—that's very close to Dallas," Hilary explained. "Six Flags is a big amusement park—rides, games, shows, and all that."

Tath hugged her to him. "This isn't a big amusement park, but I always like to go to the carnivals for old times' sake. Are there any special rides you'd like to go on?"

They had arrived at the neon arches shaped like flamingos that adorned the gates to the carnival. Hilary watched as Tath took out a few crisp dollar bills to pay the entrance fee.

"I guess I'm fairly traditional," she said shyly. "I'd like to go on the merry-go-round and the Ferris wheel, and then we'll see."

"We'll see it all," he promised as they entered the fairgrounds. "Look—there's the carousel coming to a halt right now. Shall we get on a horse or a zebra or—say, they even have unicorns."

"That's what I want—a unicorn," she said, forgetting

reality as they drifted into a fantasy world.

"Whatever you say." Tath bought their tickets, then hoisted her onto the make-believe animal's back. "You're not supposed to ride two on one animal but I slipped the man a little extra for it," Tath whispered as he clambered on in back of her. Hilary felt his strong hands close upon her waist as the calliope began its tuneful oom-pah-pah, oom-pah-pah.

They whirled around and around. The lights and decorations of the fairground, the throng of carnival-goers, all became for Hilary a colorful blur as the carousel went faster and faster in a giddy whirl. She reveled in the sense of leaving the known universe, feeling herself to be weightless, with only Tath's firm grip on her waist to remind her of her tangibility.

She could feel his warm breath in her ear, and her head felt increasingly light. She closed her eyes against a wave of dizziness and clutched the pole on which their unicorn was suspended. Tath clasped her waist and rained feather-light kisses on her neck and shoulders. Snuggling tightly against him, Hilary laughed gaily, not sure whether it was the carousel or Tath's forceful presence that was responsible for the lightheartedness she felt.

From the carousel they went on to the Ferris wheel—and again Hilary was conscious only of Tath's magnetic presence and warm embrace as they soared over the universe again and again. They bought cones of frothy pink cotton candy at a stand, and Tath licked the spun sugar from her lips in a provocative manner before pulling her to him and giving her an ardent kiss.

"Having fun?" he asked, his breath warm in her ear.

"Mm-hm," she said, leaning her head on his shoulder as they wandered up and down the midway. They laughed at their distorted figures in the Hall of Mirrors, where they spent a good half hour clowning. When they emerged, Tath asked, "Ready for the Scrambler?" and led her to one of the wilder rides.

"I'll pass on that one," she said, shuddering as she watched people strapped into cages shrieking as they were flung around vertiginously beneath the starlit sky.

"I guess it's time to win my lady a piece of plush," Tath mused, glancing at his watch.

"A what?"

"Carnie talk for a stuffed animal. Come on, let's go on to the games of skill and chance," he urged.

She let him steer her to the front section of the midway, where the game booths were lined up side by side.

"Don't ask me to shoot the ducks for you," Tath joked. "After all, they're near relatives of penguins."

Penguins. The oceanography expedition...Justin Mills. Resolutely, Hilary pushed the unwelcome intrusion of reality from her mind. She hadn't felt so carefree and happy for years, and she wasn't going to let anything spoil her mood.

"Step right up, gents," came a booming voice. "Win your pretty lady a kewpie doll or a cuddly toy in the high-striker."

Hilary gazed ahead at a booth where a man was hoisting a sledgehammer in an attempt to strike a treadle hard enough to catapult a weight to hit a gong at the top of a tower.

Failing after three tries to hit the gong, the man shrugged and handed the hammer back to the concessionaire. The latter began his pitch again, and Tath propelled her quickly to the booth.

"I'll try that," he told the concessionaire, handing him a dollar bill. He took the sledgehammer in his right hand and lifted it easily above his shoulder, then brought it down forcefully on the treadle at the base of the tower.

A shrill bell announced his success. "See that, gents?" boomed the concessionaire. "This fine fellow has won the little lady a prize." Turning to Tath, he asked, "What'll it be, sir? A giant kewpie doll or one of the life-sized animals? When you hit the bell on the first try, you get your choice of the best prizes."

Tath looked at her. "It's up to you, Hilary. It's your present."

"I think a stuffed animal," she began, scanning the row of large toys displayed on a shelf at the back of the booth.

"Oh, Tath, look!" she cried, pointing to a life-sized brown and white toy terrier. "He could be Snuffy's double!"

"Except that he can't get into any mischief like the original," Tath said, grinning. To the concessionaire he said, "We'll take that stuffed dog."

The man called to a young girl who'd been standing to one side—his daughter, Hilary supposed—and she reached under the counter for a replica of the Snuffy-like mascot. Tath took the animal and placed it in Hilary's arms.

"He's adorable," she said, delighted. "You know," she confessed shyly, "I always wanted to win one of these animals at games at the Six Flags, but I never even came close. Thank you, Tath." She stretched up to give him a quick kiss. But she found her lips lingering on his longer than she had planned, and despite the Snuffy lookalike between them, they managed a passionate kiss that sent shivers up her spine.

Only when she became aware of applause and good-natured hoots from the surrounding crowd did she break away. "He really does look so much like Snuffy," she murmured to hide her confusion as she hugged the soft animal to her.

"So much so that I'm getting nervous for my blue sweater," Tath teased, slipping his arm around her waist. "Here, let me carry him, he's kind of a handful." He took the terrier and stashed it under his other arm as they strolled away from the high-striker booth.

Suddenly, Hilary felt her knees buckle with weakness, and she realized she was famished. She had eaten nothing but the cotton candy since lunch.

Tath's firm grip kept her from collapsing. "Hilary, what is it?" he asked, his voice edged with concern. "Are you all right?"

"Yes, yes, just hungry," she said. "Could we get some hamburgers or something?"

"Sure. Say, don't tell me you didn't have any dinner. I just assumed you'd eaten at the hotel before I came. Why didn't you say something?"

"I forgot all about not having eaten," she said. "I was so curious about where we were going, and then I've been having such a good time since we got here that food just didn't enter my mind."

"Well, it had better enter your mouth, and the sooner the better," he said, piloting her toward the food concessions. He ordered double cheeseburgers and Cokes for them, and Hilary gratefully began to wolf hers down.

"Not exactly gourmet fare," Tath apologized between bites, "but I didn't think you'd last until we could drive to a restaurant."

"It's delicious," she assured him as she ate the last of her cheeseburger and drained her Coke. "Whoof—I'm stuffed!" she said contentedly.

"Me, too—I had already eaten at Mother's bash," Tath said. "I know how we can work it off, though," he added slyly.

"Please, Tath, no more rides. Not on a full stomach. I couldn't."

"Who said anything about rides? It's after midnight, anyway, and we should be getting home. I was thinking we'd go back to the boat and—"

"I don't think we'd better do that," she interrupted quietly. "Tath, I've really enjoyed this evening, and I'm so glad you thought of it, but nothing's really changed between us."

She was surprised and to her annoyance, disappointed when he didn't argue. "All right, I'll take you back to your hotel, then," he said amiably. "It's rather late to stop off at Mother's party, isn't it? But I want you to know, Hilary, that's one obstacle you don't have to worry about anymore."

"What do you mean?" she asked as they exited from the carnival through the neon arches.

"I told my mother I've asked you to marry me," he said. "We have her blessing."

She stopped and faced him. "I find that hard to believe, Tath. Unless—you told her you'd take over the mill, didn't you? Her feelings toward *me* couldn't have changed just like that."

"I won't pretend she wouldn't still prefer that I'd chosen someone like Mary Lynn Weber," he said, ignoring her reference to the mill, "but her feelings toward you *have* changed, Hilary. You see, I also talked to Hank this afternoon. I called him just after you left."

"Tath!"

"Don't worry, I didn't say anything to him about our personal relationship. But I did tell him, as head of Visual Communications, how pleased I was with your work so far, and I managed to find out a thing or two about you from him."

"What do you mean?" she asked warily.

"I mean your full scholarship to the University of Texas at Austin, where you made the dean's list every term," he replied. "And where you were also president of a certain sorority that it just so happens my mother belonged to when she was at college."

"And that's enough to make me socially acceptable all of a sudden?" she asked skeptically.

"It gives you two a common bond," he pointed out. "I guess, too, that my mother had assumed you weren't a college graduate."

"Because my father is a barber?" she demanded.

"Oh, Hilary, I know Mother seems a terrible snob. But she really isn't so bad when you get to know her. As you will when—"

"We'd better be going," she said, cutting him off. She didn't want to begin quarreling about his proposal all over again.

"We'll let Snuffy's double ride in the back seat," Tath said when they got to the Porsche. "It's somewhat cramped back there for a human, but I don't think this little guy will mind, and since he's not the real McCoy, I don't have to fear for the upholstery."

Hilary gave a rueful laugh. "I can't help missing Snuffy, though," she confessed.

"I know. Would you believe I miss the rascal myself? For all his sins, I'll always have a soft spot in my heart for him. After all, he brought us together."

"We would have met anyway," she observed.

"Sure, at my office, across a desk. It was much more

intriguing to come out of the shower and find a luscious redhead peeking under my bed," he teased, opening the car door for her.

She got into the Porsche without answering, grateful that the darkness hid the blush she felt creeping into her cheeks.

As he pulled out onto the highway, Tath said, "By the way, as I was driving out to Mother's party tonight, I thought some more about your proposal for the commercials."

"Yes?" she said tentatively.

"I like it very much," he assured her. "You did a terrific job, but there's something I'd like to discuss with you."

"What's that?" She had a suspicion even before he spoke that it would concern their disagreement over using models.

"The end, the last scene with models wearing dresses of Justin cotton. I've thought about it and I still don't want it. By the time Justin cotton gets to that stage, it's pretty much out of our hands. We sell the fabric, and I want the commercial to end in the factory with shots of the printing and dyeing."

"We can do it that way," she answered slowly. She felt so certain that the models added a good finishing touch to the commercials that she still hated to give up the idea. Choosing her words carefully, she said, "The consumer only knows the finished product. The person you've directed the commercial to, the person you're trying to sell, is the one who'll wear a shirt or dress. That's what you're selling."

He thought about it. "You really want those models, don't you?"

"I feel it's right, Tath. I have to give you my honest professional opinion."

"But it seems to turn it into a fashion show," he argued. "I'm afraid women will get interested in the dresses and forget my cotton."

She considered his reasoning. After a moment, she said, "How about one model? We'll just have one model and one dress. That way it won't seem like a fashion show or parade, but we'll still have a glimpse of the finished product."

He nodded. "That sounds better. I don't see the need for

it, but I'll trust your judgment. I prefer to have just one model."

"Good!" Relief swamped her and she wondered if part of her response was simply to his statement that he would trust her opinion.

"Everything else looks fine, and the cost seems reasonable," he said. "I'd like to get it done as soon as possible."

She felt a sense of elation. Happy that Tath liked her plans, she said, "That's good. We'd like to go ahead soon, too. I've talked to everyone—my brothers, our cameraman, the crew—and set a tentative date for three weeks from next Thursday, weather permitting. That way we'll have three weeks to get the music worked out and the props ready."

Tath looked across at her. "I'd like to do it sooner if you can work it out."

"When do you prefer?"

"Will it be possible to be ready in a week?"

She thought about the problems such a rush would cause. "I might not be able to get the cameraman in that time."

"Will you try?"

"Certainly. I'll check into it tomorrow morning and let you know. If the weather is bad, we'll pick an alternate date."

"Fine."

She had been so intent on their conversation that she had paid little attention to where they were going. Now, as she looked out the car window, expecting to see the familiar lights of downtown New Orleans, she was shocked to discover they were approaching the pier where Tath's yacht was docked.

"Tath! You lied to me!" she exclaimed. "You said you'd take me back to the hotel."

"And you took an unscrupulous privateer at his word?" he joked as he stopped the car and turned off the ignition. "I'm Sir Francis tonight, remember?"

"It isn't funny, Tath. If you think I'm going to go along with this—"

"You don't have a choice, my lovely," he interjected. "I've abducted you."

"Tath—"

"No, Hilary, let me speak," he said, suddenly solemn. "I brought you out here because we really do have a lot to talk about. I've made the decision about my future. I've decided to take over Justin Mills."

She was stunned, but all she could say was, "Then I guess we really do have to talk, after all."

In silence, they made their way to the dock together. Tath carried the stuffed dog he had won for her at the high-striker, and it seemed to Hilary that the glass eyes held a baleful look that reflected her own inner qualms.

- *16* -

THEY ENTERED THE LOUNGE, where one soft light burned. It was cool, quiet, and intimate. Hilary watched Tath step behind the bar and remove a tall green bottle of wine from the refrigerator. He uncorked it and paused a moment to unfasten his sweater and slip it off. He undid the buttons of his shirt until it was open to his navel, and she saw the dark, curling hair on his chest. It was a small, routine gesture, yet personal, the first step in undressing, and he had a casual, slightly disheveled look that added to his appeal. She watched as he poured two glasses of chilled white wine, turned the stereo low, and approached to offer her a glass.

She accepted and sat on the blue cushions of a long, built-in sofa. If only she could throw caution aside and accept Tath's proposal, she thought wistfully. Mulling it over, she glanced outside and saw the moon shining above the dark live oaks that lined the far side of the levee. Her dreamy longings changed to sensitive alertness as Tath sat down inches away, facing her.

"What are you thinking?" he asked.

"About your decision to take over the mill, of course, about where that leaves us."

"You told me to make a decision about my future and I've made it," he said. "We never discussed how you'd feel about giving up your job in Dallas, though. Would you mind?"

She thought about it. "I'd rather change jobs. Find something like this in New Orleans. It's time I worked for someone other than my brothers anyway."

"Then you don't mind staying?"

She paused and looked at him intently. "How much do you allow your mother and Elliot Compton—and Justin Mills—to run your life?"

His eyes were clear as he gazed steadily at her. "Not a damn bit, but I'd be a fool, Hilary, if I didn't find their offer attractive. That's a handsome, tidy sum that I'll never make elsewhere, and it's good, steady work."

"That's true, I suppose, but a week ago you seemed to feel so strongly about it. You sounded certain that you didn't want to get tied down to the mill."

"With that kind of salary, I might not be too tied down."

"You know better than that." She paused a minute, then added, "What's important to me, Tath, is *why* you are taking their offer."

In the depths of his eyes, something flickered. It was an almost imperceptible infinitesimal change, yet she caught it. He placed his drink on a table and reached to take hers from her hands.

His jaw was set in a determined thrust, and suddenly she wondered what he was getting ready to do. He turned around from placing her glass on the table. This time, when his gaze met hers, there was no doubt about his intention. She felt it to her toes before he reached for her.

"You think too much, Hilary."

"I have to about something this important."

His arms tightened and he tried to draw her to him. "I'll tell you what I think right now. You're frustrating, infuriating, beautiful, desirable..."

She laughed and pushed herself away. "Tath, this isn't fair. I want to go back to the hotel."

All the time she talked his mouth curled in amusement while he watched her with lidded eyes. Finally she asked, "Are you taking me home?"

"Nope."

"Tath!" She pushed forcefully and rose to her feet to move away from him.

"Come back here, Hilary!" he ordered. "I'm going to show you that you need me as much as I need you."

She tried to change tactics. "All right, Tath." She drew a deep breath as his warm lips kissed the delicate place behind her ear. "You'll seduce me..." If only she could keep her wits about her! It was an effort to talk and impossible to resist him as his mouth trailed a fiery path to the nape of her neck. He held her hair away while he kissed her, and Hilary bent her head forward.

She rested her hands against his chest and said, "You won't gain anything or solve anything. It'll be..." She took another deep breath and tried to cling to her train of thought. "...another night of love, but it won't solve our problems." Her head rolled on her slender neck and she tilted her face up to look at him. "Actually, it's cruel..."

"Cruel!" His voice startled her into sudden awareness and she looked up at him.

"Lord, talk about cruelty, Hilary," he exclaimed. "Only a week ago I viewed marriage as about the same as a permanent stint in the county jail. You've made me fall in love with you, and look at the trouble it's caused me! To top it all off—I finally decide to give up my freedom because I love you wildly, I can't live without you, and you refuse my proposal!"

"I didn't refuse."

"You didn't?"

"I can't say yes, but I haven't said no. At least not an absolute, final refusal. First I need to know why you're taking the job at the mill. If it's not what you really want, if you'd rather be on your way to Antarctica..."

His hands slipped down her bare arms to send a distracting tingle through her. His voice was husky, driving another fraction of her attention from her words. Even more disturbing was the hungry look in his eyes as he watched her. "Suppose I don't want to go to the Pole anymore, that I want to settle down and come home every night to my wife? Suppose, Hilary, I want it even if they tear up those checks— or if I tear them up?"

She studied him. "A week ago you wanted oceanography. It's just beyond me how you can change that much in such a short time."

"I fell in love that quickly." He placed his hands on both sides of her face and tilted her head up to gaze down at her. "What if I don't want to go on that expedition? Won't you give me an answer to that question?"

"I can't because I don't know the answer. I'll have to give it more thought. You were so positive..." Her words faded because she didn't want to voice her thoughts, her opinion that perhaps he didn't want to face the fact that he was only yielding to family pressure.

She caught hold of his wrists. "Tath, please take me home now. This may only make things more painful later."

He leaned down to kiss her neck. "No." The word was soft, flat, and final.

Even so, she felt she had to protest, to make some effort against the onslaught of silken caresses and fiery kisses. "You're not being fair. You're holding me against my will."

"Hmmm?" He raised his head a moment and looked at her. "How much against your will?" He leaned forward to kiss her warm throat where her pulse throbbed against firm flesh. His mouth trailed lower, his hands agile, moving, shifting, touching.

"This will only make things worse..."

"Supposing you accept?" he murmured against her ear. "If we let this opportunity go by, we'll always regret it."

She closed her eyes as he pulled her closer, into his arms. "You're hopeless," she whispered.

"But not helpless. I'm going to get an answer from you tonight, Hilary."

Startled at the conviction in his words, she opened her eyes wide to look up at him. He watched her closely and continued in a calm voice, "No more waiting. I'll get an answer before the sun comes up over the Mississippi!"

While he talked, she watched one brown hand reach for her blouse and expertly undo the buttons. Her lacy brassiere followed it to the floor, and a flash of heat went through her as his warm hands fondled the creamy globes of her breasts.

Conflicting feelings boiled inside her—anger at his persistence, and arousal from his sensuous actions.

"What kind of answer will that be?" she asked. "One given in the height of passion."

He paused and his eyes narrowed. His hands slipped around her waist and his gaze wandered lazily over her. Standing inches away from him, bare to the waist while he looked at her, she felt erotic tension engulf her.

His voice was deep and tantalizing as he said, "How can you say no, when we were meant for this?"

What was the matter with her voice? She listened to herself, the mere whisper that came from her throat, "This isn't enough for marriage—there are a thousand other aspects . . ."

With an easy movement he swept her into his arms and carried her to the sofa to sit down and hold her on his lap. She tried to catch his hands, to stop his compelling caresses. One arm held her against him while his other hand drifted down her spine, his warm, callused palm and fingertips provoking delicious currents along her back.

Her awareness diffused, shifting with kaleidoscopic patterns. She felt his warm legs beneath her, his slacks and hers a barrier between them. His hand reached the small of her back, each stroke on her sensitive skin causing a surge of pleasure. She gasped and closed her eyes.

Suddenly his fingers touched her chin and tilted her face. She opened her eyes to find him looking at her with smoldering intensity.

His voice grated as he said, "From that first meeting in my bedroom, you've been a challenge. Always, no matter what, you've dredged up that damn cool logic." His voice deepened and she felt his arm tighten slightly around her.

"Hilary, this is one night you're not going to fling reason in my face." She heard the urgency, the fierce promise in his voice.

His fingers tightened on her jaw, pressing her cheeks so her lips pouted. He leaned forward to tease them with his own. She wanted to kiss him, to open her lips to his, but his large, strong fingers held her. She felt as if she would melt with desire at the same time as she blazed with response to his escalating loveplay.

Again he startled her by suddenly placing both hands on either side of her face, making her look at him. His eyes searched hers.

"Have you ever experienced anything like this with another man?" he whispered.

"No." Her answer was immediate and sincere.

"I haven't with another woman," he stated flatly. "You're very special, Hilary. I love you beyond anything I thought possible. Don't be afraid of family pressure on us, because you have me wrapped around your little finger."

Befuddled by his words, she gazed at him. The idea of this strong, sophisticated, commanding man telling her he was wrapped around her little finger overwhelmed her, because he sounded as if he meant every word.

"Hilary, darling, will you marry me?"

Aware that she sat in his lap with her hands on his bare chest, while she herself wore nothing from the waist up, she knew what she *wanted* to say and she knew what she *should* tell him. His hand drifted down from her face, unfastening her chinos and dipping under the pale blue lace beneath to expose her honeyed flesh to his touch.

Her fingers slipped around his neck, trailing through his thick hair to rest at the back of his head. Drowning in rapture from his hands, his mouth, she squeezed her eyes closed and laid her cheek on the top of his head, feeling his soft hair against her skin. "Tath, how can I . . ."

"I can all but hear the gears shift in that brain of yours. We'll see what it takes to put them out of commission . . ."

He pulled her into his arms for a kiss that scalded, that drove her to wild abandon. While he kissed her, he unclothed her fully. She clung to his powerful shoulders, aware that he twisted and moved, peeling off his clothes until his lithe, tanned body was as accessible to her as her smooth, eager skin was to him.

Naked, her limbs entwined with his, she was overcome by an onslaught of passion that made her senses reel as Tath took incredible care to please her, driving her to surrender all restraint.

Her hands explored and caressed, eliciting blazing responses from him until the moment when she lay cradled in his arms and he rose slightly to look down at her.

His voice trembled as he asked, "Now, Hilary, will you marry me?"

It was as impossible for her to refuse him as it would be for a blossom to refuse to open to the warmth of the sun. "Yes! Oh, Tath, you got what you wanted. How can I think of anything except yes? I want you forever."

While his fingertips stroked her long, slender legs and she writhed in ecstasy, her own hands exploring his hard muscles, he spoke in a lazy drawl, "I didn't get exactly what I wanted, Hilary. Not yet."

Through heavy lids, her long lashes obstructing her view of him, she tried to fathom what he said. "I'll marry you. I'm not holding anything back..." she whispered. "What do you want?"

His answer was lost, drowned out by her moan as she sat up and reached to pull him to her, her mouth seeking him.

Awash with unbearable longing, she needed him to a degree she hadn't dreamed possible. And then he startled her by asking again, "Will you marry me, Hilary?"

He lay flat on his back beneath her. Dimly, from some far recess of consciousness, she heard his question. She lowered herself onto his chest and whispered into his ear, "Yes."

With a fluid motion that didn't interrupt his scorching kiss, he shifted her beneath him, allowing her red hair to fan across the pillow. He looked at her with eyes darkened to storm-cloud gray.

"That's what I wanted!" he whispered. "A simple, unequivocal, unconditional acceptance. No logic and no hesitation." Holding his weight off her, he whispered before leaning down to kiss her, "I'm that demanding, Hilary."

His words sent a thrill coursing through her and she pulled him down.

As he took her with ravenous intensity, her desire for

him spiraled. Finally, clinging to his hard, strong body, she heard a groan as she caressed his flat, taut muscles. He gasped and moved, their pounding heartbeats gaining intensity, drowning out all other noise until she achieved a shattering peak of satisfaction.

In time she came back to reality. Encircled in Tath's arms, she relished their bliss. On the wide sofa she lay on her side with her fingers splayed against the damp curls on his chest. While she became aware again of the cool air, the gentle rocking of the boat, the soft music in the background, he brushed the stray curls away from her face.

"Hilary." His voice was deep.

She knew what he wanted, what he had to say. She twisted to look at him. "I won't hold you to it," he told her.

She laughed. "Tath Justin, I intend to hold *you* to it!"

He rose so swiftly on one elbow to look down at her that she almost rolled off the sofa. Tath slipped his arm around her waist and pulled her against him.

He frowned. "Do you mean that? I can't hold you to a promise extracted under those circumstances, but I just had to drive you beyond that point of reasoning everything out. I want you to need me to the same extent I need you, Hilary."

She felt a rush of pleasure and placed her hand against his cheek. He turned his head to kiss her fingers and then looked at her again.

Solemnly she said, "I meant it. I love you, Tath, wherever you live, whatever work you want to do—I'm yours."

He scooped her into his arms for a kiss that threatened to destroy all of her blissful calm.

Finally he released her and gazed into her eyes. "That's why I wanted the filming of the commercials moved up two weeks—so we'll be free for a wedding and honeymoon."

She pushed against him and sat up while he lay back and grinned. "Of all the damned arrogance!"

He chuckled. "It wasn't arrogance. I'm just stubborn enough to persist. I wasn't going to give you up."

His words sent a thrill coursing through her. Anger at his self-confidence was impossible. But she had to ask, "Did you tell your mother you were planning on such an early wedding date?"

"I promise you there'll be no opposition from my mother," he answered.

She had to accept his word for it and hope for the best. She sighed and settled against him. "I hope she'll genuinely like me when we get to know each other better."

"She's already thawed considerably. Just be patient, Hilary. You won't be around her for the next month anyway, because we'll be on our honeymoon."

She turned and rose on her elbow to look down at him. His dark brown curls clung damply to his forehead. His skin contrasted darkly with the blue sofa. She could hardly take her eyes off him. How she loved him! "I suppose you have that all planned, too," she said lightly, her happiness spilling over, making her feel giddy and more fully alive than ever before.

"I might get your opinion on a thing or two—such as where you would like to go."

She smiled. "I have a feeling that's a rhetorical question and you're humoring me, but I'll give it some thought." She lay down on his arm again and snuggled close, utterly content.

He continued in a flat voice, "After we get back from our honeymoon, perhaps you and Mother can get acquainted in the time that's left before we go."

She took a deep breath. "Not only are you arrogant, you're exasperating! Where will we go then?"

"Off to see the penguins, my darling."

His words brought an explosive yelp from her and she sat up. "Tath!"

His crooked grin gave her the answer before she asked, "You're going to the Pole?"

He shoved a curl away from her cheek and said softly, *"We're* going to the Pole—if you'll go with me. I have decided to take over the mill, but I was able to talk Elliot into postponing his retirement for another year so I can go on at least this one expedition. And as you may remember, he and Mother did agree that some shorter trips would still be possible in the future. Before Elliot retires, I'll have to bring in a second-in-command anyway. Even Mother agrees that's just good business sense."

Joy, exasperation, and surprise all raced through her. "Why didn't you tell me? It would've solved everything. Tath, I can't believe you would hold back—why didn't you tell me?" she asked again.

"Darling, I told you tonight that you have me wrapped around your little finger—I wanted you to need me, to love me the same way. I wanted you to want to marry me wherever I live, whatever I do, no conditions, no ifs..."

She slipped her arms around his neck and kissed him. Finally she raised her head. "Tath, I love you so much that—"

He silenced her with a passionate kiss. Once again she lost all power to reason as she surrendered herself to the unconditional love for him that filled her heart.

____ 06864-0 A PROMISE TO CHERISH #100 LaVyrle Spencer
____ 06865-9 GENTLE AWAKENING #101 Marianne Cole
____ 06866-7 BELOVED STRANGER #102 Michelle Roland
____ 06867-5 ENTHRALLED #103 Ann Cristy
____ 06869-1 DEFIANT MISTRESS #105 Anne Devon
____ 06870-5 RELENTLESS DESIRE #106 Sandra Brown
____ 06871-3 SCENES FROM THE HEART #107 Marie Charles
____ 06872-1 SPRING FEVER #108 Simone Hadary
____ 06873-X IN THE ARMS OF A STRANGER #109 Deborah Joyce
____ 06874-8 TAKEN BY STORM #110 Kay Robbins
____ 06899-3 THE ARDENT PROTECTOR #111 Amanda Kent
____ 07200-1 A LASTING TREASURE #112 Cally Hughes $1.95
____ 07203-6 COME WINTER'S END #115 Claire Evans $1.95
____ 07212-5 SONG FOR A LIFETIME #124 Mary Haskell $1.95
____ 07213-3 HIDDEN DREAMS #125 Johanna Phillips $1.95
____ 07214-1 LONGING UNVEILED #126 Meredith Kingston $1.95
____ 07215-X JADE TIDE #127 Jena Hunt $1.95
____ 07216-8 THE MARRYING KIND #128 Jocelyn Day $1.95
____ 07217-6 CONQUERING EMBRACE #129 Ariel Tierney $1.95
____ 07218-4 ELUSIVE DAWN #130 Kay Robbins $1.95
____ 07219-2 ON WINGS OF PASSION #131 Beth Brookes $1.95
____ 07220-6 WITH NO REGRETS #132 Nuria Wood $1.95
____ 07221-4 CHERISHED MOMENTS #133 Sarah Ashley $1.95
____ 07222-2 PARISIAN NIGHTS #134 Susanna Collins $1.95
____ 07233-0 GOLDEN ILLUSIONS #135 Sarah Crewe $1.95
____ 07224-9 ENTWINED DESTINIES #136 Rachel Wayne $1.95
____ 07225-7 TEMPTATION'S KISS #137 Sandra Brown $1.95
____ 07226-5 SOUTHERN PLEASURES #138 Daisy Logan $1.95
____ 07227-3 FORBIDDEN MELODY #139 Nicola Andrews $1.95
____ 07228-1 INNOCENT SEDUCTION #140 Cally Hughes $1.95
____ 07229-X SEASON OF DESIRE #141 Jan Mathews $1.95

All of the above titles are $1.75 per copy except where noted

WHAT READERS SAY ABOUT
SECOND CHANCE AT LOVE BOOKS

"I can't begin to thank you for the many, many hours of pure bliss I have received from the wonderful SECOND CHANCE [AT LOVE] books. Everyone I talk to lately has admitted their preference for SECOND CHANCE [AT LOVE] over all the other lines."
—S. S., Phoenix, AZ*

"Hurrah for Berkley . . . the butterfly and its wonderful SECOND CHANCE AT LOVE."
—G. B., Mount Prospect, IL*

"Thank you, thank you, thank you—I just had to write to let you know how much I love SECOND CHANCE AT LOVE . . . "
—R. T., Abbeville, LA*

"It's so hard to wait 'til it's time for the next shipment . . . I hope your firm soon considers adding to the line."
—P. D., Easton, PA*

"SECOND CHANCE AT LOVE is fantastic. I have been reading romances for as long as I can remember—and I enjoy SECOND CHANCE [AT LOVE] the best."
—G. M., Quincy, IL*

*Names and addresses available upon request